Murder at Galena Gallery

A Karen Prince Mystery

By

Sandra Principe

ISBN: 0-9767954-3-4 (paperback)

Published by: Galena Publishing; PO Box 18; Galena, IL 61036.

Acknowledgements

I would like to thank everyone who has purchased my books and especially the mystery fans who have written to me. I enjoy hearing from you.

Disclaimer

Books by Sandra Principe

Murder in Galena
Murder on the Mississippi
Murder at Galena Stables
Murder at Galena Gallery

Dedication

To my brother, Frank, with love.

Chapter One

Opening Night

Friday Evening

It was May first and spring had finally arrived in the little town of Galena. All signs of winter's dreary gray had been washed away by April's showers. Now color abounded. There were dense clusters of yellow daffodils, new green grass and pink flowering crab apple trees. The red brick historic downtown was ready for the season as well. Each of the store fronts held abundant new offerings for this year's tourists.

I took Ken's hand as we entered Galena Gallery on Main Street. It was 5:30 p.m. on a gorgeous Friday evening and Ken and I were attending the opening night of Galena Gallery's Spring Show. Marsha and Ed, the gallery's owners, were welcoming the patrons, new and old, after the long cold winter.

The gallery was already crowded and it looked great.

Fifteen foot tall white walls showcased the new paintings beautifully. Spotlights illuminated art by local and national artists alike. Ken and I worked our way to the carved oak spiral staircase leading to the upper floor of the gallery.

"Come on," I said to Ken. "I'll show you my contribution to the show."

Four Seasons Bouquet (a photo of which is on the cover of this book) hung on the wall right at the top of the stairs. The large painting, 60 inches by 46 inches, was the culmination of my winter's work.

"Wow!" was all that Ken said.

"That's just the response I was going for," I said with a laugh. Even though Ken and I had been seeing each other for nearly a year now, I make a habit of not letting anyone see my work until it's finished. And this was Ken's first viewing.

"I wanted to capture a feeling of abundance and irrepressible joy," I said. "You know, the feeling you get when the warm spring sun shines on your face, and the sky is a gorgeous blue and birds' songs fill the air. You get the feeling that life is full and happy and the future is bright and hopeful. I wanted to paint that feeling in flowers," I said.

"You accomplished your goal," Ken said in a rather more serious tone than usual.

"Thanks. There are enough sad things in life. And I don't deny or ignore them. But I try to balance them with the positive. I actually feel it's an honor to be chosen to paint art like this."

Ken looked at me rather quizzically.

"I suppose that sounds rather 'other worldly.' What I mean is, the urge to create this type of work is so strong it's sort of like it chose me. When I gave up my law career to paint, I had no idea where it would lead. But I was drawn to the feeling I get in creating these works. It's like taping into a river of peace, harmony and beauty, and letting that river flow through me, through my paint brush and onto the canvas. Hopefully that feeling comes through to the viewer and brings out those same feelings in them," I said and felt myself blush.

Ken squeezed my hand. "It does. And it's beautiful," he said. "But how can you bear to part with your work?"

"I live with my work for a while, then share it, and make room in my heart to create new work. Sharing your work is part of the artist's life—part of the cycle of creating art."

A crowd had gathered around to listen and I answered several questions about my painting process and my flowers, before Ken and I continued our tour of the rest of the show.

The upstairs gallery was comprised of two large rooms of paintings and sculptures. Track lighting illuminated the floor to ceiling artwork on this level as well. Six gorgeous bronze sculptures stood on short pedestals at the top of the stairway. Ken studied the heron sculpture with its long piercing bill, curved neck and detailed feathers. The patina was a gorgeous blue gray, just the shade of a real blue heron.

"How in the world did someone make this?" Ken asked.

"If you really want to know, I can tell you," I said.

"You can?"

"Yup. It's called a lost wax process," I said. "It's complicated, but in essence, the sculptor first makes the sculpture out of clay. Then you make a plaster cast around the clay. When the plaster hardens, you cut it in half and take out the clay. Then you have a mold that you fill with wax. When the wax is hardened, you remove the mold and you have a wax version of your sculpture. At this point, you can refine the markings on the wax sculpture. Then, you attach a sprue, which is sort of like a wax stem, to the top of the wax and encase the wax sculpture in plaster again. The sprue sticks up through the plaster casing. Then you fire the plaster encased wax sculpture upside down so that the wax all melts out through the sprue hole. Now you have a perfect hollow mold of the sculpture that you want. The foundry pours molten bronze into the mold and when the bronze cools and hardens they chip away the plaster. Then all that's left to do is the finishing: refining rough edges, polishing and adding the patina," I concluded.

"How in the world did you know that?" Ken asked.

"I did some sculpture work at the Palette and Chisel Academy in Chicago years ago," I said. "I love bronze sculpture, but it's really messy work and hard on your hands. At least it was on mine."

"Well, that's quite an involved process."

"There are only a few art foundries that can do that kind of work."

"It's a beautiful sculpture," Ken said.

We studied the other bronze pieces and then made our

way around to the front gallery overlooking Main Street. We studied Johnny Lately's landscape paintings of Galena country vistas. "I love the way he lets the light glow behind the clouds," I told Ken.

"They almost have a religious feeling," Ken said.

"I get that feeling from his work, too," I agreed.

Someone behind me said, "So, do you like my new work?" I turned and saw Johnny Lately smiling at me.

"Johnny! As a matter of fact, I do. This is my friend, Ken Kruse. Ken, this is Johnny Lately," I said.

"Nice to meet you, Ken. Let me introduce my Uncle, Wilbur Lately, and his associate, Isolde Gaines," Johnny said. We chatted for a few minutes then continued on our tour.

As we turned to our right, Ken looked at the closed doorway in the corner of the room. "Where does that go?" Ken asked.

"To the third floor. It's an old apartment that Marsha and Ed converted to the framing shop for the gallery. You know that big wooden stairway in the sculpture garden behind the gallery? That's why it's there. The owner had to put in the stairway as a fire escape to meet code when the third floor was leased out as an apartment in the 80's," I said.

"I don't think I've ever seen the sculpture garden," Ken said.

"Really? You can walk out to it through the back room of the first floor gallery. Come on, I'll show you," I said and led the way back down the spiral staircase. At the bottom of the stairs, we ran into Bella Donna in her white chef's coat, tall white chef's toque, and her new signature red triangle scarf tied around her neck. Not that anyone would miss her anyway. Bella is six feet tall and, as they say, rather large boned. But now you'd always be able to tell it was Bella by her red scarf and matching red shoes. She got the idea from her favorite chef on the Food Network, Mario Batali, who always wears orange clogs with his white chef's uniform. Well, it was distinctive; I had to give her that. Bella and I met last spring when she was selected as the first winner of the Turning Points Award. Turning Points is the foundation I set up a few years ago to help other people who, like me, discover their dream late in life. The award comes with a grant to pay all of the winner's expenses for five years. That should give them time to get their business off the ground without undue financial worry. I was able to set up the foundation because, after I retired from law at 44 to pursue my own dream of painting, fame and fortune came my way in the form of a winning lottery ticket. I'm quite content with the simple country life I've chosen, so using my winnings to help other people pursue their own happiness was perfect for me.

Bella and I hugged and she introduced a 20-something-year-old young lady clad in a white coat, who carried a tray of chocolates and champagne.

"This is Destiny Smyles, my new assistant. Destiny, these are my friends, Karen Prince and Ken Kruse."

"Nice to meet you. I'm sure you'll enjoy working with Bella. And I'll bet you have some great meals, too," I said.

"Oh, I do!" Destiny said.

Whether that affirmation was in response to enjoying working with Bella or having great meals or both I couldn't quite tell.

"Try the chocolates! They're my new specialty," Bella said. "In fact, you two have to come to my new shop on Sunday. We're having a chocolate tasting event to celebrate the start of the tourist season. You'll come, won't you?" Bella asked.

"A chocolate tasting? I wouldn't miss it. You know me and chocolates! What time?"

"Anytime after noon would be great! You can make a lunch of it. I'm giving a talk about chocolate at 1:00 so try to be there then if you're interested. I'm so glad you'll be there. Hopefully, we can talk more then. I was just on my way upstairs to check on things. You know how it is on opening night!" Bella said and started up the stairs. Then she turned back and said, "Destiny, why don't you pass that tray around downstairs and then, when you refill it, come on up to the second floor with it."

"Sure, Bella," Destiny said offering us another chocolate. Ken and I chatted with Destiny for a minute and learned that she was working on her bachelor's degree in English Literature at Clarke College, just across the Mississippi River in Iowa. That gave Destiny and Ken an immediate connection, despite the contrast between Destiny's Goth black lipstick and nail polish and Ken's clean cut all American style. Ken had taught English Lit at Clarke before he retired and became a Coast Guard officer. We'd met last spring when he was piloting the boat searching for a friend of mine who'd gone overboard. But that's a whole other story.

Destiny was telling Ken about her current courses when

Marsha flicked the lights and asked everyone to gather in the first floor main gallery. Ken and I found a good spot to stand near the stairs with a view of Marsha and Ed. "I'll show you the sculpture garden later," I promised Ken.

Marsha and Ed stood next to Marsha's desk with the big spiral staircase rising behind them. They clinked their champagne glasses and Marsha said, "Welcome everyone, to the start of Galena Gallery's second year!" A round of applause filled the room. "Thank you. Thank you all. In honor of this grand event, Ed and I are giving away a $1,000 gift certificate right now! You have to be in the gallery to win so could everyone gather here in the main gallery please?" Marsha asked. "We're drawing names for the prize. You all wrote your names on the entry slips and put them in this bowl when you came in the front door, right?" Marsha asked. "Anyone who didn't, please come and do that now before we have the drawing. The bowl will be right here on this desk," Marsha said and patted the desktop next to her. A few stragglers came down the spiral staircase and joined the crowd.

"Now, can you all hear me?" Marsha asked. There were a few mumbles from the back of the crowd. "No? Ed, help me up," Marsha said, as she climbed on top of her desk. "How's this? Better?" There was a positive response, including a few chuckles and then applause. "OK! First, let me introduce our gallery artists," Marsha continued. "First, Karen Prince. Karen, can you raise your hand?" Marsha asked.

I did, reluctantly, and received a round of applause.

"Barbara Briggs, who creates our beautiful art jewelry," Marsha said. Barbara raised her hand and was welcomed by applause as well.

"And Johnny Lately, our wonderful landscape artist," Marsha said. We all looked around and scanned the room for Johnny.

"He was here earlier," I whispered to Ken. "He's the artist who introduced us to his Uncle Wilbur and his associate, Isolde Gaines."

"Johnny? Don't be shy. Please raise your hand," Marsha said. But Johnny did not respond. "Hmm—well, we'll introduce Johnny later," Marsha said and continued with two more introductions. "And now, the drawing! So, you've all put your names in this glass bowl, right? And one lucky winner will be able to add to their art collection," Marsha said.

Ed raised the bowl up to Marsha. All eyes were on them as Marsha reached into the bowl to select the winning name. Suddenly, the silence was shattered by screams from the watching crowd. The bronze heron sculpture had plummeted from the second floor and crashed onto Wilbur Lately's head. Wilbur fell to the floor as more horrified screams filled the gallery.

"Stand back," Ed yelled as people crowded toward them.

"I know CPR," Ken announced and moved toward Wilbur. I dialed 911 on my cell and called for an ambulance.

When I hung up, I made my way to Ken's side. As he performed CPR, I grabbed the table cloth from a nearby appetizer tray and applied it to the gaping red wound on Wilbur's head.

Chapter Two

Who's Who and Where Are They?

Friday Evening

Wilbur was beyond CPR. The bronze statue had killed him instantly. The gallery was abuzz with a mix of speculation, fear, horror and just plain old shock. Ed draped a coat over Wilbur and Marsha locked the gallery doors.

"Please stay calm, everyone. The ambulance will be here in a minute," Ed said. From several former encounters, I had Detective Cavanaugh's cell phone number programmed into my cell phone. I called him now, knowing he'd want to see the scene before the paramedics moved the body. He answered on the second ring.

"Detective Cavanaugh, here," he boomed into the phone.

"Detective, it's Karen Prince. I'm afraid—you need to…" I fumbled for the right words. Were there right words? I plunged in again, "Can you come to Galena Gallery right away? 106 South Main Street. Someone—Wilbur Lately, he's dead."

There was silence on the line for a moment, then Detective Cavanaugh replied, "I'll be right there. What happened?"

"We were all here at the opening and a bronze statue fell on him!"

"And you're sure he's dead?"

"Yes, I think so. The paramedics will be here any minute, but there's no pulse, no breathing, and a terrible gash on his head."

"Don't let them move him. In fact, don't let them touch anything in the gallery until I get there!" Detective Cavanaugh said.

"OK. But please hurry. There are 200 people here. Marsha and Ed have asked them not to leave but I don't know that they can stop them!"

"Right. Do your best. And Karen, I don't know why you are so often on the scene when something like this happens but leave this investigation to me! Got it?" he admonished me.

"Got it. Of course! Just, well, please hurry," I said again and hung up.

I looked at Ken. He shook his head and said, "Nothing more we can do for Wilbur now."

"What an awful accident," I said to Ed and told him and Marsha about my call to Detective Cavanaugh. "I hope you have good insurance," the former lawyer in me added.

"We do, but I don't think we'll need it," Ed said.

I looked at Ed at first not comprehending the implications of his statement. He saw my confusion and said, "Karen, this was no accident. This was murder."

"Murder!" I gasped.

"There's no way that sculpture fell on its own. Even if someone accidently bumped into it, it wouldn't have fallen over that railing. Someone had to lift it over the railing and drop it," Ed said.

I stared at Ed in disbelief. "You're saying someone did this intentionally?" The fact that we'd all just witnessed a murder rocked me.

"Exactly," Marsha said. "That's why I roped off the stairway and locked the gallery doors. Someone was up there and dropped that sculpture on poor Wilbur's head!"

The crowd was talking more now and asking each other questions.

"Did you see it fall?"

"Did you see anyone upstairs?"

"Who did it?"

"Is he dead?"

Marsha rang a bell to get everyone's attention and told her patrons that Detective Cavanaugh and the paramedics would be there shortly. "Detective Cavanaugh has asked that everyone wait here until he arrives," Marsha said.

As if on cue, Detective Cavanaugh's large figure appeared outside the front door.

"I'll let him in," I volunteered and made my way through the crowd to the front of the gallery. Detective Cavanaugh's mustachioed countenance peered back at me through the glass door. I turned the lock, opened the door and stepped aside to let him enter. A uniformed officer followed him in. "Karen, this is Deputy Stevens. He'll guard the front door. Don't let anyone in or out of here without my say so. And start a list of names of everyone here tonight," Detective Cavanaugh instructed Deputy Stevens. Then he turned back to me and said, without preamble, "Where's Wilbur?"

"Back there, by Marsha and Ed," I said. I led Detective Cavanaugh across the main gallery to the base of the spiral staircase where Wilbur lay under a coat. Ken, Marsha and Ed guarded Wilbur's body. Detective Cavanaugh stooped down beside Wilbur, took his pulse and confirmed for himself that there was nothing we could do. Detective Cavanaugh stepped back, removed a small digital camera from the inside pocket of his long gray overcoat and took photos of Wilbur, the heron statue, and the stairway.

"Karen, who owns this store?" Detective Cavanaugh asked.

"We own the gallery," Ed replied taking Marsha's hand. "Our friend, Larry, owns the building," Marsha added.

Detective Cavanaugh took out a spiral notebook from his back pocket and wrote down their names and phone numbers. Then he said, "I assume this is the statue that fell?"

"Yes, that's it," Ed said, pointing at the bronze heron a

few feet from Wilbur.

'Has anyone moved anything?" Detective Cavanaugh asked.

"No, we left everything as it was," Marsha responded.

"What about upstairs? You said this statue fell over the railing?" Detective Cavanaugh asked.

"It came from up there," Marsha said, pointing directly above us. We all looked up at the top of the spiral staircase. "But it didn't just fall. It couldn't have. Someone had to have lifted it up over the railing," Marsha said.

"You're saying this couldn't have been an accident, then?" Detective Cavanaugh asked. "You're sure?"

"Absolutely," Marsha said.

"Has anyone touched that statue?" Detective Cavanaugh asked.

"I moved it so I could get in close to Wilbur to give him CPR," Ken said.

"And so I could put some compression on Wilbur's head," I added. "But it was already too late."

Detective Cavanaugh glared at Ken and me then said, "Did anyone move anything else?" He looked around our little circle.

"No," Ken, Marsha, Ed and I all said.

"Fine. Then don't let anyone near him until the paramedics get here. Show me where this bird fell from," Detective Cavanaugh said to us.

"I'll show you," Marsha said, and led Detective Cavanaugh up the roped off stairway, with me right behind them.

At the top of the stairs, to our right, stood a row of sculptures. There was a short empty pedestal in the center of the row. "The heron was right there," Marsha said. The empty pedestal was about two feet long, one foot wide and two feet high.

"You see, the top of the heron was below the top of the railing. We liked it there because you could sort of see it through the railing posts. But the railing posts were close enough together that the sculpture couldn't fit through them. So, it couldn't have fallen to the first floor unless someone lifted it over the railing and dropped it!" Marsha said.

Detective Cavanaugh took more photos and then asked, "Who was up here when this happened?"

"No one," Marsha said. "Everyone was downstairs because we were about to draw for the $1,000 door prize."

"Well, someone was up here," Detective Cavanaugh said. "Are there any exits besides this stairway and the front door?"

"Not on the second floor," Marsha said. "But there's a stairway off the third floor that leads down to the back garden," Marsha said. "And there's the back door on the first floor."

"Show me," Detective Cavanaugh said. He turned back to me and said, "Karen, make sure that first floor back door is locked and guarded, would you? I don't want anyone coming or going until I get everyone's name."

Darn! I wanted to see that third floor exit myself! But I could see his point, so I said, "Of course," and dashed back downstairs. When I got there I found that Ed already had Bella in place guarding the back door. No one would get by her.

I raced back up the spiral staircase, through the second floor gallery, and then up the narrow stairs to the third floor to rejoin Marsha and Detective Cavanaugh.

This was my first time in the framing studio. There was a whole lot of equipment and very little walking space. I saw a large tabletop mat-cutter, a work table, filing cabinets, and supplies but no Marsha or Detective Cavanaugh. I made my way through the narrow spaces around the equipment to the open back door.

Detective Cavanaugh and Marsha stood on the small wooden balcony looking down at the wood framed steps leading to the courtyard. "The killer probably went out this way," Detective Cavanaugh said. "Maybe we'll be lucky and get a print off the door knob or this railing. Don't touch anything up here until my Deputy dusts for fingerprints."

As we reentered the framing studio, Ken came running up the stairs. "Detective Cavanaugh, the paramedics are here," Ken said between deep breaths. "I asked them to wait until you talked to them."

"Thanks," Detective Cavanaugh said and headed back down to the first floor with the three of us right behind him.

Two men that I didn't recognize had moved a gurney in beside Wilbur. Galena's ambulance service is run by volunteers so the response time is lengthened by the time it takes for someone to call them, and for them to get to the ambulance and then to get to the scene. But for Wilbur, response time had been irrelevant.

Detective Cavanaugh released Wilbur's body to the paramedics and asked one of them to call the coroner and let him know what had happened here. Detective Cavanaugh then put on gloves and bagged the bronze as evidence.

"I need to interview the people here," Detective Cavanaugh said.

"You can use my desk in the back gallery," Ed suggested.

"Fine. Send folks back to me one at a time," Detective Cavanaugh directed. "Tell Deputy Stevens they can leave out the front door after I've talked to them."

As Detective Cavanaugh was settling into Ed's desk, Deputy Stevens came to tell Cavanaugh that a man was insisting on being let in. "He says his name is Johnny Lately," I overheard the Deputy tell Cavanaugh.

"That's Wilbur's nephew!" I interjected.

Detective Cavanaugh looked at me and then said to the Deputy, "Send him back here to me. Don't let him talk to anyone until I see him."

A minute later a blue jean clad Johnny Lately was led back to Detective Cavanaugh's desk. Johnny is thirty years old, five foot eight, of slight build, with short dark hair and dark rimmed glasses.

"What's going on here?" Johnny asked, looking from Detective Cavanaugh to Marsha and Ed and then to Ken and me.

Detective Cavanaugh looked at Johnny. "There's been a…," Detective Cavanaugh paused. "I'm sorry to tell you this but your Uncle is on the way to the hospital. The paramedics have just taken him."

Johnny gasped. "Is he all right? What happened?" Johnny stood and started to leave. "I have to go to him," he said.

"In a minute, son," Detective Cavanaugh said. "Sit down here. I have some bad news. There's no easy way to tell you this. Your Uncle, I'm afraid he's dead."

Johnny's eyes widened. He collapsed into the chair next to Ed's desk.

"Where were you just now?" Detective Cavanaugh asked Johnny.

"My Uncle—my Uncle is dead?" Johnny responded.

"Yes. I'm afraid so. Where were you when this happened?" Detective Cavanaugh asked.

"I—I was walking along the river. I left to get some air. He was fine. What happened? Was it a heart attack?" Johnny asked.

"So you were here earlier?" Detective Cavanaugh asked him.

"Yes. I'm one of the artists here. I brought my Uncle to see my work. I just left for a minute…" Johnny's voice trailed off.

"Why did you leave?"

"My Uncle and I were talking. I had to leave to think."

"You were arguing?" Detective Cavanaugh asked.

"He wanted me to stop painting and take over the farm." Johnny's voice trailed off again.

I saw the look in Detective Cavanaugh's eyes and I knew he thought he'd found his killer.

"I want to see my Uncle. Can I go, now?"

Detective Cavanaugh hesitated but then said, "Yes, you can go see your Uncle. But don't go anywhere else and don't think about leaving town. I'll want to talk to you again tomorrow morning."

"I'll take you to the hospital," Ken volunteered. "You're shaken up. You shouldn't drive."

"Thank you," Johnny said.

"I'll call you," Ken said to me as the two of them left.

Detective Cavanaugh began his interviews of the patrons and I hovered nearby to hear what I could. I'd known Johnny for two years now, ever since he'd joined Marsha and Ed's gallery. I could not see that gentle soul, who painted light filled landscapes, as a killer. But someone who'd been here obviously was and I wanted to find out who.

I listened to all of the interviews, which took until 1:00 a.m. Destiny and Bella were the last to talk to Detective Cavanaugh. It turned out that Destiny was the only one in the back gallery when the crash occurred. She swore up and down that the killer was the ghost who haunted the gallery and that she'd seen him—a figure all in black, flying down the fire escape and running out the back gate.

Chapter Three

Wake Up Call

Saturday Morning

I slept fitfully Friday night. My dreams were filled with ghosts racing down flights of stairs and images of poor Wilbur lying on the gallery floor. Sometime around 8:00 a.m. I dreamt I was lying on the gallery floor next to Wilbur. Ken was wiping my face with a wet towel. The towel was scratchy. I tried to speak, to tell him to stop. I drifted to consciousness and my eyes fluttered open. Morning light streamed into my bedroom through tall glass windows. My black Norwegian Forest Cat, Truffles, stood on my pillow, meowed and licked my chin.

"Truffs!" I exclaimed. My nightmare retreated as morning light filled my eyes. I sat up and Truffs hopped down, prancing in circles and trilling.

Truffs' looked up at me with her brilliant green eyes. Her long full tail was erect and her mane fluffed out across her chest like a little lion. Norwegian Forest Cats are a large muscular breed, with a full double coat and great tufts of fur on the bottom of their paws to protect them when walking on icy fiords. Overall, they are an intelligent breed and Truffs was in the top 99th percentile. Her vocabulary was phenomenal, with a range of meows, trills, and yips to communicate her every thought, feeling and desire. Right now, she was telling me it was way past her breakfast time!

"All right. All right," I said and slipped on my slippers. I grabbed my terry cloth robe from the back of my closet door and made my way to the stairs leading to the kitchen. On the landing, I glanced up at the spiral staircase leading to my studio. I definitely wanted to get into my studio this morning. I knew it would be hard to paint after last night, but I needed to do something to take my mind off the shock of Wilbur's murder. I was working on one of my favorite subjects, an orchid painting, and maybe that would help. I figured I could get in a few hours of work before I had to be at the Galena Art Museum—the GAM, as we locals called it.

Dara Brown, the GAM's Board Chairwoman, had organized a joint fundraiser between GAM and The Galena Humane Society. Galena residents would bring their pets to the event and local artists would sketch or paint the pets' portraits. The proceeds would be shared between the two organizations.

I walked down to the kitchen and looked out the kitchen window to see blue sky and the thermometer already reading 60 degrees. At least that boded well for a good turnout. I just hoped I could concentrate on painting after everything that had happened last night.

Truffs pranced in front of the pantry then took her position in front of her food dish. In this portion of our morning ritual, I opened the pantry and selected a can of Fancy Feast Salmon and Shrimp then placed the contents on one of Truffs' eating plates. Yes, Truffs does have her own set of dishes decorated with little mice running along the edges. She's definitely a pampered pet, but it hasn't spoiled her a bit!

Once Truffs was happily eating her breakfast, I poured myself a cup of steaming java and thanked the inventor of the timed coffee pot. Simple pleasures are wonderful. I sipped dark, strong coffee and moved into the living room to watch the birds at the feeders as I finished my morning cup.

Goldfinches flitted to and fro. Their drab olive winter plumage had been replaced with their namesake brilliant yellow-gold. The garden along the edge of the deck brought a smile to my face. Deep blue grape hyacinths intermingled with pale blue scilla to form a dense carpet of flowers. Bunches of early daffodils sprang up in their midst, their white petals and orange centers glowing in the morning sunlight. It would indeed be a glorious day to be outside.

I went back to the kitchen, popped an English muffin in the toaster, poured myself a second cup of coffee and breakfasted outside along with my feathered friends. After Truffs and I were both properly fueled, I toured my gardens. I try to do that every day, even if just for a few minutes.

As part of my tour, I gathered a beautiful bouquet from

the gardens. I've found it's best to collect flowers in the morning when they're at their freshest. The trick is to bring the water-filled vase into the garden with you so the flowers are out of water for the shortest possible period of time. Making the bouquet right there in the garden also has the benefit of selecting each bloom at precisely the stage and coloration I'd like for my bouquet. I reveled in the effects of light dancing on and through the petals and took note of which flowers would bloom soon. I always select flowers that are in bloom as well as some that are in bud so that my bouquet includes the anticipation of future garden joys. I selected golden crocuses, cream colored daffodils with pink trumpets, white daffodils with golden-orange centers, and lilies of the valley. I then collected fragrant boughs of lilacs from the tall bushes along the south side of the house.

The spring breeze blew through my hair and the sun warmed my face. It was a good day to be alive. The strong clear notes of the phoebe filled my ears and brought a smile to my face. A bluebird pair fluttered around one of the houses Ken had built last fall. He'd installed a bluebird trail along the perimeter of my 100 acres. The pair sent flashes of dazzling color with their blue wings and orange breast feathers as they considered one of the boxes for their spring nesting site. The bluebird of happiness—aptly named, I thought, because each bluebird sighting brings an irrepressible smile to the lucky viewer.

Now, arms filled with flowers and heart filled with the sights and sounds of spring, I had pushed last night's tragedy far enough into the background to enable me to paint. I headed inside to my studio.

I live in an old farmhouse with an attached silo that holds

a circular stairway leading to my studio. I had the studio designed to maximize the dramatic light I like on the floral arrangements that I paint. The studio has a sixteen foot tall peaked ceiling with a long wall of seven foot tall north windows. There are other windows in the room, but when I paint, I have them covered with blackout shades so that natural light illuminates my still life arrangements from a single direction, the upper left.

Right now, I'm working on a painting of a white orchid with a crimson center. The initial studies started with thumbnail sketches—small, three inch by two and a half inch pencil studies in my sketch book that just focused on overall light and dark patterns and the large overall shapes of the painting.

When I was happy with the thumbnail concept, I did a one-quarter linear scale study in watercolor. The oil painting will be 24 inches by 20 inches so the watercolor study was six inches by five inches. Creating a scaled study lets me think more about the position of the blossoms I will use to carry the viewers' interest throughout the painting. When I was happy with the scaled study, I did a full sized pastel study. That was several days' work in and of itself, but it's essential to see the design and scale of the painting before I move on to the oil. The oil painting might take two weeks to complete, even painting every day. So I figure that the time to do a good design study is a worthwhile investment.

The key to a successful painting starts with the design— the "why" of the painting. You need to stay with the design until it takes your breath away with its power, grace and beauty. Every element of the painting must work together to form a seamless whole. The shadow supports the light; the arching leaves lead the eye. Every element: color, composition, values—all must work together to support the concept of the painting—the reason why you chose to paint this particular artwork.

Today I'm working on the heart of light of my painting—the white orchid blossoms at the center of the panel. The Dutch painters used something called "color houding"—the use of color to emphasize form. The white flowers in the light will naturally come forward. The darker color passages, like the leaves in shadow, will naturally recede and so emphasize the form of the plant or bouquet that I'm painting.

I arranged little piles of paint on my palette in their usual order. Placing the colors in the same position on my palette lets my hand move to the correct color without searching for it when I'm painting. That's one of the little tricks to staying in the thought-free state of "flow" when painting is at its best. Music is another aide to staying in the flow. I turned on my CD player and let Jean-Pierre Rampal's rendition of Luigi Boccherini's flute quintets transport me as I studied my first blossom.

Flower by flower, the orchid painting took shape. Three hours flew by in what seemed like minutes—or really, seemed like no time at all. It was only the musical overlay of *Froggy Night* emanating from my cell phone that brought me back to awareness of anything other than my orchid and the paint on my canvas.

I glanced at my watch—Noon! I grabbed my cell phone and looked at the display. It told me that Galena Gallery was calling so I flipped open the phone and said, "Hello Marsha!"

The silence that greeted me told me this wasn't Marsha after all.

"Hi, Karen. It's Johnny."

"Sorry, Johnny. I thought you were Marsha. Oh, I am so sorry about your Uncle." I sunk into my studio chair and swirled away from my painting. My mind went back to last night's horrible tragedy. "Johnny, is there anything I can do for you?"

"Actually, I'm calling to ask for your help," Johnny replied.

"Of course. What can I do?"

He hesitated and then said, "The police think I killed my Uncle. I didn't do it, Karen. I loved him. We'd disagreed on things but I certainly didn't—I wouldn't—," his voice trailed off.

"Of course. Of course you wouldn't. But I'm not sure what I can do," I said.

"You can find out who did this," Johnny said.

"I'm sure Detective Cavanaugh will find out who really did it," I reassured him.

"Karen, the problem is that he thinks he has. He thinks it's me!"

I was silent for a moment while I thought about this. What was I supposed to do? He sounded so desperate and alone. I took a deep breath and said, "Of course, I'll do what I can to help. But I'm not a detective. I can't make any promises, Johnny."

"I know. But you're good at finding out the truth. I heard what you did last summer, at Galena Stables. And I heard about the other two cases you solved. I need someone I can trust, Karen. Someone who believes I'm innocent. Please, just do what you can. That's all I ask."

"Of course," I assured him.

"Marsha told me how you helped Detective Cavanaugh in the past," Johnny said.

"I don't know that Detective Cavanaugh would call what I did helping him," I said.

"Well, I would. I really need your help, Karen. There's no one else I can turn to," he said. "You don't know what this means to me. Thank you."

"I'll do what I can, Johnny. I promise."

After we hung up, my mind bounced between thoughts about the importance of my promise to him and concerns about what in the world I could do to help him. I sat like that for some time. When my thoughts returned to my surroundings, I realized I was late.

I hurriedly put my palette in the small fridge I keep in my studio for storing paint and cut flowers. The cool temperature preserves both of them between painting sessions. I wiped the excess paint off my brushes with a paint rag and then washed my brushes in my studio sink with good old fashioned Murphy's Oil Soap. I'd banned toxic cleaning solvents from my studio years ago and learned from an article I'd read that oil soap worked wonderfully on brushes. I carefully rinsed the soap out of my brushes, dried them with a towel and then reshaped them with my fingertips before laying them between two clean towels to dry and stay dust free. A lot of work, I know, but worth it to keep the shape of my painting tools just right.

Then I jumped into the shower and did a quick change for the afternoon's GAM event. I'd selected jeans, turtleneck, and a washable over-shirt for the occasion. Painting outside can be messy. Aside from a makeshift and unfamiliar painting environment, you have to contend with wind, bugs and, hopefully, crowds. One of my painting buddies once said, "I have two kinds of clothes—those with paint on them and those about to get paint on them." I figured jeans and an old shirt were a good choice for the day.

Next I gathered my painting equipment. I grabbed two painting panels and the pouchard box that I'd packed yesterday afternoon. A pouchard box is a wonderful invention for the traveling artist. It's the artist's equivalent of an executive's briefcase. The wooden box opens to reveal an attached, slide-out paint palette. Below the palette, you can store paints, brushes and a painting rag. The lid is two inches deep with grooved slots to hold painting panels. You can lock the lid in place at a 90 degree angle to the palette. In that configuration, the box becomes an easel to hold the panel in place for painting. There's even a place at the bottom of the box to screw in tripod legs so the box can stand on its own like a regular easel, or you can skip the legs and set it on a table or your lap. Handy dandy! I was set to go.

Little Truffs was curled on her blue rug in the sun in the living room and blinked sleepily when I called her name to say goodbye. She stood, did a kitty-yoga stretch, then curled up again on her rug.

"See you later," I said and left her to her feline dreams.

The Boxster, my little silver sports car, awaited me. I backed into the drive and pressed the batmobile button. The black fabric roof folded back and slid under a metal panel leaving a sleek silver profile. I loved this car and the day was perfect for a drive. As I headed down Blackjack Road, the sun shone down and spring air whipped around me.

This first weekend in May the willows were a haze of warm yellow-green against the cool azure blue sky. Lavender lilacs covered 15 foot tall bushes planted years ago around old farmhouses. An indigo bunting flitted across the road ahead of me, its iridescent blue feathers shimmering in the sunlight. Blackjack Road mostly rides the ridge tops, twisting and turning the full 11 miles into town.

Galena is in the very northwest corner of Illinois. It's unglaciated, meaning that the glaciers never leveled it off as they did almost everywhere else within hundreds of miles. As a result, we have rolling hills and valleys, offering long vistas of contoured farmland, woodlands, and sightings of the critters who populate them including: opossums, raccoons, wild turkeys, deer, coyotes, groundhogs, foxes, cute little skunks, a few bobcats, red-tailed hawks, bald eagles and a host of song birds. There are some snakes, too, but I try to avoid those sightings. Thoreau would have loved Galena's countryside. Sunlight and shadows fell in tree patterns across the road as I wound my way into town.

The Galena Art Museum, the GAM, is located right off Highway 20 next to the Galena River. The building's red brick matches the 19th century red brick used in 95 percent of the buildings on Galena's downtown Main Street. Strict historic regulations insure that Galena's downtown district looks as it did in its 1860's heyday. In fact, 90 percent of Galena's downtown is actually on the Historic Register.

I pulled into the GAM's already crowded parking lot and

pressed the batmobile button again to put the top up on my little Boxster. Much as I love dogs and cats, I don't want them making themselves at home on the Boxster's leather seats.

Then, pouchard box in hand, I headed to the GAM. The pet painting event was located on the grassy lawn along the banks of the Galena River just outside the Galena Art Museum. Dara Brown, chair of the event, stood beneath an arch of colorful balloons marking the ticket and registration booth. One of Dara's assistants sat at a table accepting entry fees and checking in artists and patrons.

"Karen!" Dara said when she saw me, then gave me a big hug. "We have you set up right over there," she said as she pointed to one of a dozen tables situated on the lawn. "People will purchase a ticket for a pet portrait here and then bring you a card like this," Dara said as she waived a purple index card in the air. "And Mike will be coming around with his camera to take any photos you'd like of your subject. He'll print them out for you, too, so you should have everything you need. The pets are supposed to sit for their portraits, but the cats and dogs may not see it that way. We figured we'd have a photo backup just in case."

"Thanks. I usually paint from life but in this case, a photo could be a lifesaver. It's either that, or I could do an abstract painting," I laughed. My painting style is highly realistic so the thought of my doing an abstract made Dara laugh as well.

"Come on, I'll walk you to your table. Need any help with your equipment?" Dara asked.

"It's all right here," I said as I patted the pouchard box

hanging from its strap across my shoulder.

As we moved away from the entrance, Dara whispered conspiratorially, "So, what do you think about Johnny and Wilbur?"

"He called me this morning," I said, shaking my head.

Dara's eyes widened and she stared at me.

"Johnny, Dara. Not Wilbur. Johnny called me."

"Oh, right. Of course," she said, her eyes returning to normal size.

"So, what did he say? Did he confess—artist to artist?" Dara asked.

"Quite the contrary. He said he didn't do it and asked me to help find out who did! He thinks that Detective Cavanaugh has him pegged for the killer and he doesn't know what to do about it! That's got to be scary and he's just lost his Uncle, who's been like a father to him," I said.

"What did you say?" Dara asked.

"I felt so sorry for him, what could I say?"

Dara nodded in silent understanding. Then she put her hands on her hips and said, "I know Johnny through GAM exhibits. He doesn't strike me as violent in any way. In fact, his landscapes are just the opposite." She paused for a moment then said, "Anything I can do to help, you can count on me."

"Thanks, Dara. Actually it would be really helpful if you'd keep your ear to the ground—or the grapevine—or whatever that saying is. You know what I mean. If anyone's got their finger on the pulse of this town it's you. And in a town this size, someone must have an idea of who dropped that bronze on poor Wilbur and why," I said.

"Actually, I've already heard a few things," Dara said.

"What? Tell me!" I said.

"Well, Oliver, the Sheriff's dispatcher, is our security guard at the GAM today. He told me that Johnny's right. He is Detective Cavanaugh's number one suspect. Johnny stands to inherit Wilbur's home, his land and his company. Detective Cavanaugh's going to see Wilbur's partner, Isolde Gaines, today. You should talk to her, too," Dara said.

"That sounds like a good idea. Do you know anything about her?"

"I don't know her very well. She's an engineer working for Wilbur at Prairie Fuels. You know that Wilbur retired from Chicago Engineering three years ago and moved out here full time to set up Prairie Fuels, right? From what I hear, Isolde was on Wilbur's team at Chicago Engineering. About two years ago, she was given an involuntary early retirement and she came out here to work with Wilbur," Dara said.

"Did they get along well?" I asked.

"I hadn't heard that they didn't. But like I said, I don't know her personally. She's sort of a loner. She's single, I know that, and she works a lot from what I hear. She has a house out on Horseshoe Mound Road, just down from Wilbur and John-ny's," Dara said.

"I'll call her. I don't know if she'll talk to me but it

would be a good place to start. Anything else you've heard?" I asked.

Dara hesitated, and then said, "Oliver told me that Johnny had been arguing with his Uncle right there at the gallery. It's hard for me to imagine Johnny arguing with anyone, but apparently several witnesses said they overheard them in the back gallery. And then Johnny leaving like that! Well, you have your work cut out for you, Karen," Dara said. "Speaking of which, here comes your first subject."

Chapter Four

Pet Painting Party

Saturday Afternoon

Ken and Baxter were walking toward us. Ken had a purple index card in one hand and Baxter's leash in the other. Ken is six foot two inches tall, with a strong erect bearing. He wore blue jeans, a white tee shirt and a navy jacket.

Baxter, his English Mastiff, weighs 210 pounds and when he's standing on all four paws, his head comes up to Ken's hip. If you consider that Baxter weighs about the same as a six foot two inch tall man, you get an idea of how solid Baxter really is. He has a powerful barrel chest that I can just barely fit my arms around. Baxter is a tawny beige color with deep brown eyes, black muzzle and long ears. He has a large strong head and can be really intimidating even though, in truth, he's a lover not a fighter.

If Baxter stood on his hind legs he'd be looking down at me. The good news is that he graduated at the top of his class in obedience school. Thank heavens!

"Ready to paint Baxter, here?" Ken asked as he came up and gave me a smile and a quick kiss.

"Sure!" I said, returning both his smile and his kiss. "I was just going to set up at this table. You remember Dara, don't you?"

"Of course. Hi, Dara," Ken said.

"Good to see you, Ken. But I'd better let you all get down to business. I need to get back to the gate and greet our guests," Dara said.

"Talk to you later," I replied.

"Good to see you again, Dara," Ken said.

I swung my pouchard box off my shoulder and onto the paper covered table in front of me. "Let's see. Baxter could sit there," I said, pointing to a grassy spot in the sun next to the table.

"Come on, guy," Ken said. "Get ready to be immortalized."

As Ken positioned Baxter, I set up my easel and arranged my panel, paints and brushes. I hadn't painted anything but flowers for eons, and I wished I'd brought some charcoal with me for sketching. Charcoal is much easier to erase and change than oil paints. Oh well. I steeled myself. It was all for a good cause.

My qualms disappeared as I began painting. With a few quick lines I put in the central axis of Baxter's head and body.

The parallel lines marking the position of the eyes and nose followed. Then, with transparent brown, I blocked in the overall body shape. The right side of my brain, the creative side, took over, and I was no longer thinking but rather moving in the flow of the painting.

Ken occasionally coaxed Baxter to stay, but he was really being a good boy. In about an hour, I had the basics for a rough but credible likeness. This reminded me of my portrait painting sessions at the Palette and Chisel in Chicago, long before I moved out here to Galena.

I was blocking in the background when someone caught my eye. A woman, who appeared to be somewhere in her sixties, dressed in a long, flowing red dress and heavy black boots stomped past us muttering to herself. She shot narrow-eyed glances at the artists and curled her upper lip revealing her teeth. People were giving her a wide berth as she made her way through the crowd.

I had just watched her pass by when Mike came up and took several photographs of Baxter. "I'll go get these printed out and have them for you within the hour," Mike said. "I've got some good close-ups of his head and a couple good overall shots."

"Great," I said. "I think it's time for us to take a break. If I'm gone when you get back, just put them under my pouchard box here, all right?"

"Got it," he said.

"Mike, do you know who that lady in red is?" I asked in a lowered voice, looking toward the woman who had circled back past us and was now ranting something about galleries' unfairness to artists.

"Oh, that's Zay Lately," Mike said. "I see her at a lot of outdoor art fairs."

"Did you say her last name is Lately? Is she any relation to Wilbur and Johnny?" Ken asked.

"I hear she used to be married to Wilbur but that they were divorced years ago. I guess that makes her Johnny's aunt, sort of," Mike said.

Ken and I looked at each other.

"Really? Thanks, Mike," I said.

"No problem," Mike replied and headed back to the GAM's office to download and print out the photos he'd taken.

Looking around now, I saw several other portraits in progress. Laurie was painting a white Persian curled up on a blanket. How un-catlike, I thought and then realized it was a very life-like stuffed toy! Probably the only way she could get a cat to pose under these conditions, I thought.

At the table next to Laurie, Suzanne was painting a petite black and white toy fox terrier, who was as cute as he could be. At about five pounds, he was a perfectly formed miniature, the sort of dog you could carry around in a large purse.

"Hi there, Suzanne!" Suzanne and I had met at the last GAM event, a show of work by high school art students. She had won the First Place award for her portrait of her father. She had a great deal of talent. Interestingly, Suzanne planned a career in medicine, as a surgeon.

"Hi, Karen. This is Max," Suzanne said, smiling. Max pranced, yipped, and took in everything around him. To say that Max was sitting for his portrait was using the term very loosely. Baxter stood next to the table and Max approached him without hesitation. Even standing on the table Max was shorter than Baxter. But both of their tails were wagging furiously. And Max didn't seem to be concerned by the disparity in their sizes. He yipped at Baxter, defending his table or saying hello, I couldn't tell which for sure. Neither pooch seemed to think size mattered. They sniffed noses and other relevant parts, and then Baxter let out a howl that stopped everyone within 100 yards. Crouching, then springing up, Baxter clearly wanted Max to come down from the table and play. Max's owner came running up to the table and laughed when she saw what was going on.

Across from Suzanne, in the center of the row of artists, Bella had set out a table of yummy looking treats. I spotted her standing behind the table clad in her white chef's toque and jacket, her signature red triangle scarf tied around her neck. We made our way over to her and she enveloped me in a giant hug.

"Come and try some of my cookies. Notice no chocolate today. Cats and dogs can't eat chocolate, you know. But I'll make up for that tomorrow at our Chocolate Tasting!" Bella said.

"I hope you all will come too," Bella said to Suzanne.

"Now, this end of the table is for pet owners and the other is for pets," Bella said. "But if you get them mixed up, it won't do anyone any harm," Bella said with a smile. Ken and I selected fruit tarts for ourselves and an assortment of biscuits for Baxter. We were enjoying our treats when Marsha and Ed joined us.

"Hey, Karen and Ken! We were hoping to find you here," Marsha said. "I have a favor to ask. There's a couple who'd like to meet you and see your studio. They're very interested in your *Yellow Orchid* painting at the gallery. I know how you value your privacy, Karen. But they're real nice folks and patrons of the arts who love to meet artists and see how they work. Would you mind? I promise it won't take more than half an hour," Marsha said.

I looked at her and asked, "Who are they?"

"Greg and Cinda Books. He's a financial consultant. Actually, he was Wilbur's accountant. I've known him for years. They're from Naperville," Marsha said.

I still hesitated. I really did guard my studio privacy. I don't even invite Ken in to see a painting before it's completed. I have a sneaking suspicion that somehow I'd be influenced by other people's judgments if they saw my work on the easel.

"Please," Marsha added.

I was such a pushover. "All right. But no comments on my work in progress. Comments on anything finished are fine," I stipulated.

"Done," Marsha said. "I'm sure they'll understand. They really are interested in the process," Marsha reassured me.

"That'll be fine. I actually love talking about the process and completed paintings," I said.

"I'll set it up for Monday, if that's all right with you. Greg and Cinda are out here for the week," Marsha said.

"How about 10:00 a.m.," I suggested.

"Count on that unless you hear otherwise from me," Marsha said.

Zay Lately marched by us again and seemed to be even angrier when she saw Marsha. Zay stopped, pointed her finger at Marsha, and said, "Now are you happy? This is all your fault!" and then stormed off.

"What was that about?" I asked Marsha.

"I don't know," Marsha said but then hesitated and added: "A few weeks ago, Zay brought me her paintings and wanted me to show them in the gallery. I told her I didn't think our gallery was the right place for her work. Really, Karen, they're all just solid black canvasses. How am I supposed to show that? But she's blaming me for squelching her career! I told her she needed to go to a modern art gallery, but I doubt they'd show her work either. Who'd want to deal with her?" Marsha said. "I only talked to her at all because of Johnny."

"Does Johnny keep in touch with her?" I asked.

"I don't think Johnny or Wilbur saw much of her after the divorce five years ago. But she's still his aunt and Wilbur's ex-wife," Marsha said.

There was an awkward silence so I changed the subject. The one that sprang to mind was our upcoming group trip to St. Barths.

The trip to St. Barths was a special treat, on my part, to celebrate Marsha's selection as the second Turning Points Award recipient. Marsha had started Galena Gallery after a career in hospital administration. But art was her real passion and this sort of mid-life career change was just what Turning Points Foundation was established to foster. Bella and her assistant, Destiny, were coming because Bella was the first Turning Points winner; Marsha and Ed, because Marsha was this year's winner; and Ken, because, well, just because. St. Barths is my idea of a dream island. It's in the French West Indies, in the Caribbean, near St. Martin, and has a perfect beach temperature all year round.

"Hey, are you all packed for Wednesday?" I asked.

"I can't believe we leave for St. Barths then! We still have a ton to do before we go," Marsha said as she looked at Ed and then back to Ken and me. "At least we know the gallery will be in good hands. My sister, Vici, and our landlord, Larry, will watch the gallery while we're away," Marsha said.

"My nephew, Christopher, who's a chef in Aspen, is flying in to watch my new shop. He's between the ski and summer seasons in Colorado so he's spending some time in Galena with me," Bella said.

"Talking about having a ton to do, we've really got to run. We're meeting some folks at the gallery," Ed said.

As they went on their way, I felt a vibration in my jacket pocket and the loud riveting sound of frogs. Ken looked at me as I pulled my cell phone from my pocket.

"I wanted a ring tone I'd recognize as mine," I replied to Ken's unasked question. I hurriedly unzipped my pocket and flipped open my cell phone before it kicked over to voicemail. I got it on the third ring, just in time.

"Hello," I said, and pressed the phone to my ear trying to hear over the surrounding chatter.

"Karen, it's Johnny. Someone's broken into my Uncle's lab," he said without preamble. "I thought you should know right away."

"What do you mean? When did it happen?" I asked. I pressed my free hand over my other ear to block out the sounds of the GAM fair all around me.

"I'm not sure when it happened. I guess it must have been last night. I just went out there an hour ago and someone had obviously rifled through his office desk. Detective Cavanaugh's taking fingerprints right now. Karen, this should show him that someone else was after my Uncle. Not me, right?"

"Right. Well, maybe," I fudged. "Johnny, who has access to your Uncle's lab?"

"Just him, and his partner, of course, and the people who work there. That's it, as far as I know."

"Who do you mean, precisely?"

"Well, Isolde is his partner. And they have someone who comes in and does some typing and filing for them sometimes. And there's Ben. He comes in and cleans the lab once a week. Just sweeps the floor and empties the trash, stuff like that," Johnny said.

"Did you call Isolde?" I asked.

"She's here. She found the mess first. I got here just after she did and the papers were everywhere. I called Detective Cavanaugh right away," Johnny said.

"You caught me at a GAM event. I can be there in half an hour," I said.

"The police aren't letting anyone in. There's really nothing that you can do here. I just wanted you to know."

"Okay. Tell you what, let me talk to Isolde, okay? Do you have any idea what someone might have been looking for in your Uncle's office?"

"I don't have any idea. He didn't have anything valuable out there, at least not that I know of. Just plants. Microscopes and stuff like that, his equipment, but all of that's still there," Johnny said.

"If you think of anything that might be missing, let me know," I said.

"Okay. I'll find Isolde for you. She's in there talking to Detective Cavanaugh. I came outside to call you, but the signal should still work inside," he said.

A few minutes later, Isolde was on the line. "Isolde, Karen Prince. I know this must be a difficult time for you. I'm so sorry for your loss. But I'm sure you'll want to find out who's responsible for Wilbur's death. And Johnny's asked me to help him clear his name. So, I was wondering if I could talk with you. Could we meet later this afternoon?"

"I don't know how long I'll be here with the police and I have an appointment at 4:00 p.m. today," Isolde said.

"Well, how about tomorrow?" I asked.

She hesitated but finally agreed.

"How about at Bella's new coffee shop at 1:30 p.m.? Would that work for you? I promised I'd be there for her chocolate tasting event and we could talk there," I suggested.

"Fine. I'll see you then. I have to go now and make sure these detectives don't make any more of a mess of my work than someone already has," she said.

"Thanks, Isolde. I really appreciate it," I said and rang off.

Ken and I decided to call it a day for the pet painting project. I packed up my things and Ken carried the wet painting. "Let me take it and do a little more work on it, all right?" I said.

"It looks great to me, but you're the artist. So, take your time. Whenever you say it's done, I'm sure I'll love it. How can I not? It's Baxter painted by you," Ken said.

I smiled. "It'll fit laying flat in the boot," I said. The Boxster has two trunks, one under the front hood, called the boot, and one in the back, called the trunk. The engine is enclosed in the middle of the car, behind the driver's seat, inaccessible to all but a Porsche mechanic. Rather exotic but it does give me more room to carry things in my little two-seater.

We had just packed my gear in my car when it dawned on me. "Oh, I never got the photos that Mike was printing out for me. I'll just run back and find him. I'll talk to you later, and see you at Bella's at 1:00 p.m. tomorrow, all right?" I said.

"Sounds good. I'll see you then," Ken said. "And thank you for the portrait."

I gave Ken a kiss goodbye, rubbed Baxter's head, and went back to find Mike. Along the way I pulled the check I'd written in advance out of my purse and handed it to Dara at the entry gate. Winning the lottery had its advantages and being able to back two of my favorite organizations was one of them.

I found Mike and collected several great shots of Baxter, then drove home.

I spent the evening packing for St. Barths. Truffs watched from her throne (a/k/a my chaise lounge) as I put bathing suits, sarongs, flip-flops and a paperback mystery in my carry-on suitcase. You don't need many clothes to lie on the beach. And after this weekend, it would be great to get away. At least I thought it would.

Chapter Five

Chocolate, Chocolate Everywhere

Sunday

I awoke early on Sunday morning and spent the first few hours of the day giving my orchids their weekly watering. A Hawaiian orchid grower once shared the secret of her success with orchids with me (besides raising her orchids in Hawaii). Her motto was "weekly, weakly". By that she meant you should water your orchids weekly with a dilute fertilizer solution for three out of every four weeks. The fourth week you use plain water to flush the chemical buildup out of the potting bark. That weekly watering, together with sun, air and gentle praise, are all that orchids need to produce spectacularly elegant flowers that last for months.

Usually, my Sunday orchid routine is a relaxing time for

me. I listen to NPR while I bring each plant to the sink for watering and check its growth and overall health. Today, however, I kept thinking about poor Wilbur and Johnny. At first I thought the break-in at Wilbur's lab had to be related to his murder. Now I wasn't so sure. If whoever broke in knew that Wilbur was dead, then they must have been looking for something valuable in the lab. That would explain the drawers being pulled out in Wilbur's office. On the other hand, if the burglar didn't know that Wilbur was dead, they could still have been trying to find something, or they could have been trying to frighten or harass Wilbur. I needed to find out more about who might have had a grudge against Wilbur. I figured I could ask Isolde when we met this afternoon at Bella's coffee shop.

I got my little notebook from my purse and added "Wilbur's enemies?" to the list of questions I wanted to ask Isolde.

It was 9:00 a.m. by the time I'd finished my orchids and I spent the next three hours in my studio on *Light on White Orchid*. Three hours was typically enough time to block in three flowers. Each of the flowers would have three layers of paint: the block in, the refinement, and the detailing. I'd spend the next week or so on the orchid blossoms themselves. There'd also be the leaves, stems, vase, background and all the fun little insects and butterflies. Like most serious undertakings, it would be accomplished step by step, or in this case, stroke by stroke and petal by petal. I didn't like letting a day go by without putting in at least three hours in my studio, and it felt good to have gotten some studio time in today. I rolled my chair back away from my easel and studied the developing painting to consider which flowers I would add next, deciding on an opening blossom and two buds. Then I washed my brushes and tucked away my palette until tomorrow.

By 12:30 p.m. I was in the Boxster heading into town to see Bella's new coffee shop and meet Isolde. The events of the past 36 hours ran through my mind as I shifted gears on the rising and falling hills and twists and turns of Blackjack Road. Fifteen minutes later I took a left onto Highway 20, crossed the Galena River bridge and turned right onto Galena's Main Street. The Galena River runs along the east edge of town and was at the top of its banks. For many years the spring thaw had caused the Galena River to overflow its banks. It had actually flooded downtown Galena stores and homes before the city created a grass covered berm and installed the 20 foot tall green flood gates at the south end of town. Every few springs, the giant gates are closed to save downtown Galena from flooding when the mighty Mississippi's waters rise so high they backflow into tributaries like the Galena River. Today the gates stood open, ready to be called into action if the waters crept any higher.

I took a right onto Commerce Street, and tucked the Boxster along the levy wall. Flowering crab trees were in full bloom, presenting a row of soft pink blossom-clouds. It was a two block walk from here to Bella's coffee shop on Main Street, but this was one of the few downtown parking areas exempt from the three hour limit. Besides, I figured that walking a few blocks was probably a good idea before attending a chocolate tasting.

Bella's new store was on the west side of Main Street, directly across from Galena Gallery. Most shops opened at noon on Sundays so tourists were already carrying packages as they made their way up and down Galena's historic Main Street.

Many of the two and three-story red brick buildings were built in the 1800's and retain their original exteriors. Bella's building was a classic. Originally constructed as a dry goods store, it had been converted to a bakery in the 1980's. Bella had purchased the bakery equipment and lease from the retiring owners this past winter, with part of her grant from the Turning Points Foundation. In Galena, most shop leases are up in March and a surprising number of them turn over in what's called the Galena Shuffle. Merchants switch shops looking for the best position they can afford to lease for the new season. They move in March, decorate and stock inventory in April and open for the new season by May first.

"Bella's Coffee, Chocolate and Catering" was hand painted in red letters outlined in gold on the large storefront window. Three round oak tables were positioned in the window and I could see that Bella already had a crowd inside. Nearly all of the tables were filled and more people stood holding cups and plates. I stepped up to the door and read "Free Chocolate Tasting Today" printed on a yellow sign. That would explain the crowd.

I had my hand on the doorknob when I heard the crash. I turned toward the sound of shattered glass and heavy impact. A small red car had jumped the curb and run into Galena Gallery's front window!

I ran across the street to find Marsha. She was just coming out of the gallery.

"Are you and Ed all right?" I asked.

She gave me a hug and said, "We're all right, thank

heavens!" We looked over at the crumpled car and watched Zay Lately climb out of the driver's side and stumble away down the street.

"Oh my God!" Marsha said.

"You'd better go inside and sit down," I said.

We told Ed who we'd just seen and he put his arm around Marsha. "We'd better call Detective Cavanaugh," Ed said, then got him on the phone and explained what had happened. Detective Cavanaugh said he'd be right there.

"Has Zay ever threatened you before?" I asked Marsha.

"Oh, she said some crazy things but I didn't think she'd do anything like this" Marsha said.

"Well, be sure to tell all of that to Detective Cavanaugh. I have to go meet Ken and Isolde over at Bella's," I said hesitantly.

"Go. We'll be fine here. She's gone and Detective Cavanaugh will be here in a few minutes," Marsha said.

"Are you sure?" I asked.

"Of course," Ed said.

I went back outside and saw that a crowd had formed around the crumpled car. I made my way across the street to Bella's and found Bella standing behind a table in the center of her store. There were two silver trays lined with handmade chocolate truffles in little brown paper cups. Boxes of assorted truffles were stacked on either side of the trays. Destiny, whom I'd met last Friday at the gallery, was behind the register ringing up sales as fast as she could. Apparently the car crash was no competition for free chocolate.

It looked like Bella's season was off to a great start. I'd had her truffles before and I was sure that, after trying one, her customers would be leaving here with a box or two to take home.

I headed over to Bella and Destiny and let them know that Marsha and Ed were all right. I was about to try a chocolate when I spotted Ken at a table along the far wall, away from the window.

"Karen!" Ken called out as he stood and waived to me. Bella looked up from her conversation with the next customer and gave Ken a little wave and a smile. I made my way across the room to Ken. He stood, gave me a warm kiss and said, "Looks like Bella has a winner here."

"It does! But Ken, didn't you hear that crash?" I asked.

"I heard something. What was it?" Ken asked.

I told him about Zay Lately driving her car into Galena Gallery.

"Is everyone all right?" he asked.

"No one at the gallery was hurt, thank heavens, but they were pretty shook up. Zay took off down the street so I don't know for sure about her. But I assume she's not too badly injured since she ran," I said.

"Karen, do you think she could have been there Friday night and dropped that statue?" Ken asked.

"I'd just started wondering the same thing," I said. "I suppose it could have been her. Apparently, she's got a grudge against Marsha and the gallery for not showing her work. Maybe she was getting revenge on her ex-husband and the gallery at the same time," I said.

"You have to tell Detective Cavanaugh," Ken said.

"He's on his way over to the gallery right now. So, he'll know shortly," I said.

"That's good. Maybe you'd better rest a minute and have a chocolate after all that," Ken said.

"Maybe I'd better," I said. "And Bella's are extraordinarily good."

"Karen, have you ever met a chocolate you didn't like?" Ken kidded me.

"You have a point. I confess. I'm a chocoholic and I intend to enjoy every bite! And Bella's really are exceptional. You'll see for yourself in a minute," I said.

"Speaking of which, I exercised great restraint waiting for you. How about if I get us a sampling now?"

"Wonderful," I said.

While Ken went to get our chocolates and coffee I used the time to scan the room. The walls were the original exposed red-orange brick. Bella had draped the ceiling with three foot wide bright orange and blue banners running the length of the room. It reminded me of Christo's extraordinary environmental artwork where he draped buildings in fabric just this shade of orange. The decorations lent a cheerful atmosphere, perfect for a shop specializing in chocolates.

Ken returned in a few minutes with a tray brimming with

treats. "Here's our lunch! I got us chocolate covered cherries for appetizers, molten chocolate torte for our entrée and chocolate-chocolate chip cookies with a side of chocolate truffles for dessert," Ken said.

"My hero," I responded as he arranged the plates and mugs on our table. "A chocoholic's dream come true!"

As we ate our dreamy confections, Bella rang a bell to get everyone's attention. A young man on her staff took over the truffle table.

Bella spoke loudly, saying, "I want to thank everyone for coming today. For those of you curious about these confections, come join me at the back of the store. I've made a Power Point Presentation about chocolate making. I'll show it on the overhead screen there. We've set up a Wi-Fi center, so you can have your coffee and catch up on email, news or just browse the web."

"Wow! I'm impressed," I whispered to Ken.

"I hope seeing how chocolate's made doesn't put us off them. You know what they say about sausages," Ken said.

"No. What do you mean?"

"The saying is that you won't want to eat sausages once you know how they're made," Ken said.

"I think we'll be all right with chocolates," I whispered back.

The crowd at the back of the store quieted as Bella began, saying, "This is just a five minute summary of a process that takes months in real life."

I looked at my watch and whispered to Ken, "That's good, because Isolde should be here in 15 minutes."

"We'll have to keep an eye out for her," Ken whispered back.

Bella projected images on the screen showing each step of the chocolate making process and read the explanatory text: "Chocolate starts from the seed pods of the cacao trees. The pods grow directly on the tree trunks and farmers harvest the pods by hand with large hooked blades. The pod's thick outer shells are hacked open with a machete and the pulp and seeds are scooped out, put in piles, covered with banana leaves and left to ferment. The fermentation process is key to developing the chocolate flavor and takes anywhere from three to nine days to complete.

"The fermented seeds are dried in the sun on bamboo mats then sent to shipping centers in burlap sacks weighing 130 to 200 pounds. Buyers inspect them for proper fermentation and then buy them from the farmers.

"Once at the chocolate factories, the seeds are sorted by type and country of origin, cleaned and weighed so they can be blended in the proper proportions for the specific flavor the chocolate maker desires. This is similar to the blending of grapes practiced by many vintners to produce a balanced wine.

"Next, the seeds are roasted at 250 degrees in large ovens for 30 minutes to 2 hours to release the flavors, similar to the way coffee beans are roasted. Roasting turns the beans a deep brown color. Then a winnowing machine cracks the thin shells leaving only the inner seed kernel called the nib.

"The nibs are ground by heavy steel discs producing a

thick paste called chocolate liquor. Some of the chocolate liquor is reserved to be used later and some is pressed to separate the cocoa butter from the solid cocoa.

"That reserved chocolate liquor is mixed with condensed milk, sugar and the separated cocoa butter to finally form chocolate in its raw state. Then it is churned until it becomes what's known as chocolate crumb.

"The crumb is rolled through steel rollers to produce a fine chocolate paste. The paste is then blended in vats for up to six days in a process called conching. The rolling and conching give chocolate its silky texture. Then the refined chocolate is tempered by repeatedly warming and cooling it so the finished chocolates will have a nice gloss and melt in your mouth.

"The tempered chocolate is shipped in liquid state to candy manufacturers who mold the chocolate into the candy treats you know and love. Like my truffles! So now that you know how this wonderful chocolate is made, go and enjoy it!" Bella concluded. There was a round of applause and Bella took a bow.

We turned back toward the front of the store and I saw Isolde coming through the door.

"I'll find us another table," Ken said.

"I'll get Isolde and find you," I said. I recognized Isolde from the gallery opening Friday evening. She'd been talking to Johnny and Wilbur when Johnny had introduced us. Isolde was tall, about five feet ten, I guessed. She had chin-length brown hair threaded with gray, which she pulled back and tucked behind her ears. She wore simple black pants and a brown sweater. "Isolde, thanks for coming. Ken is getting a table for us," I said.

"I only have a few minutes," Isolde replied.

"Fine. I'll be brief. I just want to know if there's anyone you think might have had a motive to kill Wilbur," I said as quietly as I could. "But please, let's go sit down where we can talk more privately." Isolde followed me to the table Ken had secured for us. After Isolde was seated, Ken brought us all coffee and more chocolates and Isolde seemed to relax a bit.

"I'm sure this is awfully hard for you. I'm sorry to ask you about something so painful. But it might really help find out who did this," I said.

"I'm all right. What do you want to know?" Isolde asked.

"First, tell me a little bit about what you and Wilbur were working on, would you?" I asked.

Isolde leaned toward me and said, "Wilbur had started Prairie Fuels to find an alternative to corn based ethanol. A lot of people around here are invested in corn ethanol, so this didn't make him very popular," Isolde said.

"Why did he want to find an alternative to ethanol?" I asked. "I thought ethanol was an alternative fuel and was a good thing."

"Of course, it is. But right now, ethanol is made from corn, which takes a great deal of fertilizer to grow, and uses our best farm land. That makes less corn available for food and drives the prices up all over the world. Wilbur and I figured, why put food in our cars when we have prairie grasses that grow wild and have longer growing seasons and don't require fertilizer?"

"Sounds like a good question," Ken said. "I'd heard that scientists were working on using switchgrass as an alternative to corn for making fuel," Ken added.

"Yes, they are," Isolde said. "But to offset 20 percent of our country's gasoline use with ethanol, which is one of the government's stated goals, would take 25 percent of US cropland out of food production if we're using either corn or switchgrass. Plus, it is presently much more difficult to make ethanol from the cellulose in switchgrass than from the starch in corn. A group of researchers found that using Miscanthus grasses would only take about 9 percent of farmland to produce the same amount of ethanol. That's because Miscanthus has a much longer growing season than corn or even switchgrass. It produces leaves six weeks earlier than corn and stays green until October in Illinois, long after the corn has stopped growing. Plus, it grows in marginal soils so it may not even need to compete with corn for cropland. That's what Wilbur and I were working toward," Isolde said.

"So you were growing Miscanthus?" I asked.

"We were improving Miscanthus," Isolde said. "We're making it useable for biofuel. You see, when cows eat grasses, they use an enzyme in their stomachs to turn the plant fibers into simple sugars. We isolated the gene that makes that enzyme. We put that gene into the DNA of the Miscanthus plant and now we have a grass that can be turned into simple sugars when the enzyme is released. The simple sugars can then be converted to ethanol to power cars and trucks," Isolde said.

"If the enzyme is in the grass, what stops it from digesting the plant and turning it into simple sugars when it's growing?" Ken asked.

"That's a very good question. In fact, that was the final key to making this work. The enzyme is stored in a vacuole of the plant cell. A vacuole is a special part of the plant cell that stores waste. When the grass is harvested and the cell structure is broken down, then the enzyme should be released and do its work," Isolde said.

"That seems almost impossible," I said.

"Not at all. It's already been done for corn. The corn used for ethanol is called Spartan Corn III. It has three gene splices that make it more useable for ethanol. There's a gene taken from a microbe that lives in hot spring water that cuts the cellulose into large pieces. Then there's a gene from a fungus that takes the cellulose pieces and breaks them into sugar pairs. The last gene is from a microbe in a cow that separates the sugar molecule pairs into simple sugars. Then the simple sugars can be fermented into ethanol," Isolde said. "What we have done is taken this idea and found a way to use it with a grass that has much better production capacity than corn. This is the step that should really make cellulosic ethanol a viable replacement for gasoline."

"Wow. Do you think this work had something to do with Wilbur's murder? Was there someone else, some competitor, who wanted to stop him?" I asked.

"I don't think a scientist would resort to killing another scientist. And I don't know anyone who was working on this project, at least not taking the same approach we were," Isolde said.

"Do you have any idea who else would have wanted to kill Wilbur, then?" I asked.

Isolde thought for a minute and then said, "There is someone. I hadn't thought about him in years. Not since I left Chicago Engineering. And it's been so long, I don't really think he would have done this. But he's the only one I know of that had anything against Wilbur," she said.

"Who? Who do you mean?" I asked.

"Well, his name…hmm… I can't remember. But he was on our team—the team Wilbur headed at Chicago Engineering. And this fellow was let go. He'd been a problem for the group and from what I heard he'd been a problem in other groups before Wilbur's. But when the company let him go, I know he blamed Wilbur. They actually had a memo out about it in the company, telling employees not to let him into the building." Isolde said.

"And you don't remember his name?"

"I'll think of it," Isolde said as she closed her eyes and tilted her head back. It's just that it's been three years. Oh, I've got it. It's Reilley, Ron Reilley. That's his name," Isolde said. "Last I heard he'd lost his job, started drinking and his wife divorced him. I haven't heard anything else about him after that," she concluded.

I looked at Ken. "Can you track him down on the internet?"

"I can try," Ken said. "The White Pages or Google Search may turn up something. Depends how far off the map he's fallen, I suppose."

"Do you think he's still in Chicago?" I asked Isolde.

"Don't know. But he might be. He had two kids, so maybe he stayed in the area to see them, assuming his wife still lives there," Isolde said.

"But think about it," Ken said. "If this Ron Reilley killed Wilbur, why would he have gone through his office the next day? That doesn't make sense. He'd already have had his revenge."

"That's true. Could he have gone through the office earlier, on Friday maybe?" I asked Isolde.

"Well, we all left the office about noon on Friday. So it's possible," Isolde said.

"Did Wilbur ever talk about Ron Reilley?" I asked Isolde.

"He did when we were at Chicago Engineering. Reilley had sent him threatening letters. But Wilbur hadn't said anything about him recently, at least not to me. Maybe you should check his emails or talk to Johnny," Isolde said.

"Sounds like a good idea. I think I'll do that. How did your meeting go yesterday afternoon? Who did you say you were meeting with, again?" I asked.

"I didn't. But if you must know, I was meeting with my lawyer. He's filing a patent for me for the process I was just telling you about. I can't say anymore than that until the patent is approved."

"Wouldn't the patent be in Prairie Fuels or Wilbur's name? Wasn't it his company?" I asked.

"Wilbur agreed that whoever made the breakthrough would get the patent. And I did, so the patent will be mine. Of course, once it's approved, I'd give a license to Prairie Fuels to make the ethanol with this process and Wilbur's company would make money that way," Isolde said.

"Did you tell Detective Cavanaugh about Ron Reilley?" I asked Isolde.

"No. How could I have? As I said, I just remembered about him now," Isolde said.

"I'll call Detective Cavanaugh and tell him. He'll probably want to talk to you," I said.

"I'll be around and he has my cell number. But I have to go now or I'll be late," she said.

"Thanks, Isolde. We really appreciate your time," I said.

We said our goodbyes and Isolde left. Ken and I looked at each other.

"Sounds like we'd better find this Ron Reilley. He could be our guy," I said.

"Why don't you call Cavanaugh and let him find Reilley?" Ken suggested.

"Good idea," I said and dialed Detective Cavanaugh. There wasn't a minute to lose. Detective Cavanaugh took the information I gave him and said he'd look into it, telling me once again to leave the investigation to him. Right.

After the phone call, Ken and I headed back to my place. As we walked through the door the phone rang.

Chapter Six

Best Laid Plans

Sunday Evening

I picked up the phone on the third ring, just before the answering machine got it. "Hello," I said.

It was Burt Castle calling about our trip on Wednesday. Burt is a former airline pilot who started his own charter flight business here a few years ago. He'd flown me to the horseshow in Asheville last summer and I was finding flying with him to be a much easier way to travel than using the major airlines. Burt's airstrip was just a mile from my house and his schedule was very flexible. Winning the lottery did have its perks.

"Well, there'll be six of us: Ken, me, Bella and Destiny, and Marsha and Ed. Seven, counting you," I said in answer to his question.

"If we leave early, I can get us there in time to catch some afternoon sun at the beach," Burt said.

"That would be great. Have you thought about my offer to spend the week there with us, as my guest?" I asked.

"I sure have and I'd love to. I've never been to St. Barths before."

"Well, you'll love it. It's a French Island, and the food is fantastic. It's very relaxed. Just bring your swimsuit and shorts. No one gets dressed up there at all. And the restaurants and hotels are staffed by happy young French kids just out of college. They're having the time of their lives spending a few years in the French West Indies learning about the hospitality industry. They love tourists and their *joie de vivre* is contagious. You don't see the poverty on this island that you do on so many of the Caribbean Islands. Pretty much everyone there's having a good time," I said.

"Sounds great. I look forward to spending the week there. Thank you," he said. "Oh I checked out the St. Barths airport online. Apparently, pilots need a special license to land there. But we can land on St. Martin and charter a smaller plane to fly us in to St. Barths. It won't add an hour onto our fly time," Burt said.

"Could you arrange for the charter?" I asked.

"Sure. No problem," Burt said. "From what I hear flying into St. Barths is a pretty unique experience. There's only one runway and with the prevailing winds the only approach is through a narrow pass in the mountains. You have to come through the mountain pass and then drop down pretty quickly. The runway is only 2,133 feet long. It's one of the shortest in the world and it ends at the ocean," Burt said.

"I remember landing there and that sounds about right. I guess that's why only small planes can land on St. Barths and the pilots need a special license. The good part is that it keeps the island from getting too touristy. That and the fact that they have a height restriction on buildings. They don't allow anything over two stories, so there isn't any high-rise congestion. The island is edged with a series of scalloped bays with one or two hotels on each bay. And there are wonderful casual restaurants. Like I said, you'll love it. I'm so glad you're joining us!" I said.

"I am too. Be sure to tell everyone to pack lightly. And we'll meet at the airstrip at 7 a.m. I'd like to get an early start if that's all right with you."

"Fine by me. I'm sure everyone will be happy to trade an early wake-up call for landing in time for Mai Tai's on the beach!" I said.

"Sounds great. I just wanted to touch base with you, Karen. So, I'll see you and your guests at the airstrip on Wednesday morning. I'll take care of the arrangements for the charter from St. Martin to St. Barths," Burt said.

"Wonderful! See you then," I said.

Ken and I spent the next half hour talking to and leaving messages for the rest of our group about our travel plans.

"I'm a little concerned about leaving Johnny this week," I confided to Ken. "I promised I'd help him and now I'm taking this trip. It feels like I'm bailing on him," I said.

"Well, you'll be available by phone. And, you have to remember, you have friends who've been planning and counting on this trip for months. They've arranged their schedules and they're all excited about this. I don't think it would be right for you to cancel it now," Ken said.

"I guess you're right," I agreed.

"Think how much this will mean to everyone. And it'll be good for us to spend a week relaxing as well. We've never spent a week together, and I'm looking forward to it," Ken said as he squeezed my hand.

I smiled back at him and said, "Me too."

"Well, I'd better head out. But I'll be back here tomorrow morning for the goat tour," Ken said.

"The goat tour! I almost forgot," I said.

Just as Ken was about out the door the phone rang again. "Just a sec, let me see who this is," I said to Ken.

Dara Brown's melodious voice greeted me. "Karen, go glad I got through to you. I've just heard the most incredible thing and I knew you'd want to know."

"Really? Is it about Johnny?"

"Well, yes, in a way. I heard from a very reliable source, whom I cannot name, that Bull Skittles' finances are stretched pretty thin. He's sunk a lot of money into the feasibility studies and conceptual plans for the big development that he and Johnny are planning on Wilbur's land."

"Whoa! What big development are you talking about?"

"I thought you knew! Johnny has been working with Bull Skittles for the past year. They've been making plans for a big tourist development on Wilbur's land. There'd be a Midwest Native American museum, a shopping center and a hotel," Dara said.

"But Johnny doesn't own the land." At least he didn't, I thought, but couldn't bring myself to say that out loud. I paused. "What did Wilbur think of all that?" I asked.

"At first Wilbur was dead set against it," Dara said and then paused. "I guess I shouldn't have put it quite like that. I mean, he hated the idea. Wilbur felt that the land was farmland when Wilbur bought it and farmland when he managed it, and he wanted it to stay farmland. On the other hand, he intended to pass the land on to Johnny, so Wilbur kept trying to talk Johnny out of the idea. But Johnny kept after him and I think at some point Wilbur reluctantly agreed. But he changed his mind a number of times about agreeing to the development," Dara said.

"Did Wilbur know that Johnny was still working with Bull Skittles?" I asked.

"Yes. That's why Detective Cavanaugh has Johnny in his sights as the prime suspect. I thought you knew about this."

"I knew Detective Cavanaugh thought Johnny was responsible, but I didn't know about the real estate development plan. Wow! That does not look good for Johnny!" I said and walked back over to the sofa and sat down.

"Johnny never mentioned this to you?" Dara asked.

"No. Unfortunately not. But, I suppose it doesn't matter. I mean, I don't think he did it, even if he and his Uncle did disagree about developing their farm," I said.

"There was a lot of talk about that development in town. They hadn't applied for any permits or anything like that so it wasn't in the newspaper. But they'd spent enough money on studies and drawings that a lot of people knew what they were planning. And a lot of people were against it. Horseshoe Mound is one of the most scenic areas around Galena. The thought of it becoming a shopping center didn't sit well around here," Dara said.

"I see. Well, thanks for the information, Dara. I'll have to talk to Johnny and see what he has to say about all this."

When I hung up with Dara, I filled Ken in on what she'd told me.

"Well, that doesn't mean he's guilty," Ken said.

"No, but it doesn't help his case, either," I said.

Chapter Seven

Studio Tour

Monday Morning Painting Session

I was jolted awake by blood curdling cries. It was pitch black. I sat up in bed, held perfectly still and listened intently. The sounds were coming from somewhere down the hill from my house. The cries turned into high pitched yips. A pack of coyotes had just killed some prey. I hated that sound. I know, I know. It's nature. But I couldn't help wishing they weren't such blood thirsty creatures. And they sounded so joyful about their kill. I pulled the covers up around me and snuggled in with Truffs. She didn't like the coyotes any better than I did.

"It's all right," I assured her as she nestled against me. I hit the light on my bedside clock and read 4:00 a.m. The witching hour. Why do these sorts of things always happen at 4:00 a.m.?

I hadn't been able to fall asleep until midnight last night, probably the result of having eaten about a pound of chocolate for lunch yesterday and then skipping dinner. This coyote wake-up call wasn't going to help.

I tossed and turned until 5:00 a.m. and then gave up any pretense of sleep and worked out instead. By 7:00 a.m., when Ken arrived, I'd already done 40 minutes on the elliptical machine, my Body Electric exercise tape, and showered and changed. Truffs had found watching all this early morning activity to be a real treat. Of course, she'd be taking catnaps all day.

Ken was coming over early to help Tony with our new goat herd. Actually, the whole idea of getting goats was Ken's idea. He'd succeeded in talking me into getting a herd of 16 black and white Pygmy Goats, a few weeks ago. Tony and Ken were still working out the logistics of care, feeding and housing these new critters. We'd had a steel-sided pole barn put up for them. That was an amazing experience in and of itself. Do you know they can put up a 60 by 120 foot barn in three days? And Tony was thrilled with the new structure. Now he had a proper home for the machinery he used to care for my 100 acres of land. Without the barn, those coyotes I heard last night would be feasting on my new little charges.

Anyway, it turns out these goats are cuter than cute. We'd toured a neighbor's goat farm and, between their advice and the breeder's, we'd learned a lot about goats. It turns out that Pygmy Goats are native to the Cameroon Valley of western Africa. Their official name is African Pygmy Goats. They were imported to the United States from Europe about 50 years ago. Originally they were just in zoos, but private breeders acquired them and they've really taken off in popularity. That's in part because they're fairly smart. With an IQ of 60, they quickly learn their names and will come individually when you call them for milking. At least that's what I'm told. One of the other things that amazed me was that the newborn goats, kids, I guess you call them, are able to walk within an hour of being born. Not that my new goats had already had kids, but they would, and I was looking forward to the experience of seeing the little newborns.

Pygmy Goats range in size from 16 to 23 inches at the withers (which is what you call their shoulders) and usually weigh between 40 and 70 pounds. The little babies are only 2 to 4 pounds at birth, and a doe usually has 1 to 3 kids at a time. The goats come in black, white, and tan colors. I went to a goat website and learned that there are actually names for the colors. The website said: "Agoutis range from silver-gray to black, with dark solid stockings. Caramels range from white to light brown and have light vertical stripes on the front of dark stockings. Solid Blacks are, well, solid black. Blacks are also black but can have another color around their eyes, ears and nose."

Goats are surprisingly finicky about their food. It has to be very clean or they won't eat it, which sort of surprised me. I was told we'd have to have a hay holder because if the hay touched the ground the goats wouldn't eat it. Guess it's nature's way of protecting them from eating tainted food. And here I thought goats ate anything and everything. I've learned that they're considered browsers not grazers, so their natural food is shrubs like blackberry bushes that grow up off the ground. Yes, they eat woody things like that. Of course, they need a constant supply of clean water, too.

We'd found our goats at a farm off Clarke Road outside the

Galena Territory. We'd been riding along and saw these adorable little creatures walking along inside a fence line. Ken fell in love with them, and the next thing I knew I was buying a herd of them. It turns out they're very social creatures. You can't have just one of them or they'll be extremely lonely and unhappy.

They produce a surprising amount of milk for such little animals, about a half gallon a day per milking goat. The males are called bucks (or wethers if they've had certain parts removed) and the females are called does. You have to keep the bucks away from the does, we were told, so Tony and Ken built a separate fenced area for the bucks within the larger fenced area for all of the goats. The fence has to be about 3 or 4 feet high, with two stands of barbed wire above the mesh fencing and one down low at ground level to keep out the coyotes and wild dogs.

We learned that goats like to sleep on a wooden platform, so Tony and Ken had built a number of those. Today's goat project was to build a milking stand.

When Bella heard about the goats she and Ken came up with the idea of making a local goat cheese. That increased the number of goats we decided to get from the original 4 to the 16 we now had.

By the time Ken arrived at 7:00 a.m. I was ready for a cup of coffee with him. After he went off to work with Tony, I headed to my studio, knowing I had only two days before the St. Barths trip. I spent two wonderful hours on my orchid painting, working on the newly opening buds. Time flew by studying the transparent petals, the way they overlap, the veining, and the glorious red lips, capturing all of that in my painting. When I'm painting, each brushstroke is a discrete statement. I load the appropriately sized brush with the precise color and amount of paint so that the stroke will match the shape, color and form of the part of the petal being depicted. Each visual observation, such as the bit of light on the edge of the petal, is translated into paint. I had my brush loaded with sap green paint and was just about to paint in an arching stem with a twirl of my brush when the door bell rang. I looked at my watch and saw it was already 10:00 a.m. Greg and Cinda had arrived precisely on time.

I put the loaded brush on my brush rack and dashed down the winding staircase that connects my studio to the rest of the house. Truffs was already on kitty alert, ears up, green eyes peering at the front door from her spot on the yellow sofa. But she held her ground. Truffs was a very brave kitty.

I swung open the front door, caught my breath and said, "Hello," to Greg and Cinda.

"Karen, thanks for having us out here," Greg said. "This is my wife, Cinda."

"So nice to meet you. Come on in," I said, stepping aside so they could come into the foyer. Cinda immediately spotted Truffs, who gave one of her best trills. It was love at first sight for both of them, which is very unusual for Truffs.

"Is this a Norwegian Forest Cat?" Cinda asked as she walked directly over to Truffs.

"She is. Not many people know about the breed. You must love cats," I said.

"Oh, I do," Cinda said, crouching down in front of Truffs

and giving her black silky coat a stroke. "I have three Forest Cats of my own, actually."

"You're kidding! I've never met another Norwegian Forest Cat owner!" I said.

"Well, I'd call myself more of a provider than an owner. I provide them with a home, meals, clean litter, and endless cat toys," Cinda laughed. "I don't think you can really own a cat. They'll just let you live with them if they like you," Cinda said with a smile.

"I know exactly what you mean," I said. "And I only have, I mean, I only live with one!"

Greg seemed as taken with Truffs as Cinda was. They were both on their knees admiring her highness and Truffs loved every minute of their attention.

"Marsha tells me you'd like to see my studio. But, can I offer you something to drink first? Coffee or tea, maybe?"

"Tea would be lovely, if it's not too much trouble," Cinda said.

"How about if we do our tour first and then sit down and have our tea?" Greg suggested. "If that's all right with you, Karen. I can't wait to see your studio and I'm sure we'll have lots of questions we can talk about over tea afterward. Would that suit you?" Greg asked.

"That would be fine with me," I said. "Follow me and I'll show you what I'm working on right now. The only thing I ask is that you not make any comments on the painting in progress," I said. "It's sort of a rule of mine," I said.

"I can respect that," Greg said.

"Of course," Cinda said.

We said goodbye to Truffs and I led them up the winding staircase to my studio.

"Wow," Cinda said. "I don't know what I was expecting, but not this!"

"Well, I had the studio designed for perfect light and lots of space," I said. "I spend a great deal of my life in here and my surroundings influence how I feel, and how I feel affects my work. Not that you have to have a great studio to create art, but I find it helps," I said with a smile.

My studio is long and narrow, about 30 feet by 20 feet, with a very high ceiling. The north facing wall is mostly tall windows, starting at five feet off the floor. "The windows give me a single, high, light source so that I can paint from life without huge changes in the light throughout the day. For example, if my windows were west facing, I'd have no light on my subject in the morning and intense light that changed angle as the day went on," I said.

"Do you ever use artificial light? I've talked to some artists who use daylight adjusted bulbs in their studio," Greg said.

"I have those in the two reflector lights over there," I said pointing to a corner of my studio. "But I only use them when I absolutely have to paint at night. I really prefer the cool, diffuse natural north light. I find the spot lights create a glare that's a bit distracting when I'm painting," I said.

"Can you tell us a little bit about your painting process?" Cinda asked.

"Sure. Let's see. I guess I start with the inspiration for the painting. That might come from a beautiful color, an elegant form, a certain light pattern, or an idea, like capturing the feeling of abundance and joy of a great large bouquet. Once I know what I want to convey in the painting, then I can design the painting to best present that concept to the viewer."

Cinda and Greg looked at me. I wasn't sure they'd understood what I meant so I said, "Here, I'll show you a painting from my drying cabinet and give you an example of what I mean."

I pulled open the center-folding wooden doors on the right side of my studio closet. The closet is lined with long wooden shelves painted a subtle gray-green, the same shade as my studio walls. The top shelf was empty except for two, ten by eight inch panels that were leaned against the wall. The lower three shelves held my collection of still life objects. There were birds' nests and butterflies as well as a good assortment of glass and silver vases.

I reached in and lifted one panel by its sides, then showed it to Cinda and Greg. "I finished this painting a few months ago. It's drying now so I lean it toward the wall in this closet to avoid getting dust on it. In a few more months I'll varnish it and then send it off to the gallery in New York."

"How long do you wait before you varnish a painting?" Greg asked.

"Usually four to six months. But if I'm doing a commission or have to send off the painting before then, I use what's called retouch varnish. You can use that as soon as the painting's dry to the touch, usually in a few weeks. That will protect the painting for about five years. Then the owners should have the painting varnished with final varnish."

"That's a gorgeous piece," Cinda said.

"Oh, thank you. I call this *Light on Purple Orchid*," I said.

"What was the concept for that painting?" Greg asked.

"It's the intricate color pattern on the orchid blossoms. The more you look at it the more it captures your attention. It's hypnotic," I said.

"Thanks for sharing your studio with us," Cinda said.

"You mentioned a commission. Do you accept commissions?" Greg asked.

"I do, quite a few, actually. I enjoy the interaction with clients and, since it takes months of work to complete a painting in this highly realistic style, I don't complete that many paintings each year. This way the client knows they're not only getting a painting, they're getting the exact painting that would be perfect for them," I said.

"How does a commission work? I mean, how do you work with someone who wants to commission a painting?" Greg asked.

"Well, the first thing someone should do is to look at my other paintings at one of my galleries or on my website. Then think about the paintings you like best. For instance, are you drawn to the quiet meditative feeling of the orchid paintings or the joyful feeling of abundance of the bouquets? Then we talk about size and the kind of flowers we'd have in the painting. I say 'we' because it seems like a joint project when I do a commission. Then I do a few small studies, called thumbnail sketches, which show in very miniature form what the subject and composition of the painting might be. We talk about the thumbnail sketches together and pick what we like best in those. Then I do a pastel study the actual size that the oil painting will be. Once the pastel is approved, then I do the oil painting," I said.

"That sounds like an interesting process," Greg said. He looked at Cinda.

She nodded and said, "It does. It would be wonderful to have a commissioned painting."

"Would you consider doing a commission for us?" Greg asked.

"I'd be delighted. You two think about whether you'd like an orchid or a bouquet and we'll go from there," I said.

"Thank you," Greg and Cinda said in unison.

"Well, thank you. Now, how about some tea? I'll be happy to answer any other questions you have," I said.

"Great!"

We headed back down to the living room and they played with Truffs while I made our tea.

"Here we are," I said carrying in the tea tray. I placed it on the glass table in front of the yellow sofa. You can sit there with Truffs if you'd like," I said as I poured three cups of decaf green tea.

I took my cup and saucer and sat across from them. "So, Marsha tells me you're from Naperville."

"Yes," Cinda said. "We're looking at a second home in the Galena Territory but we have to keep a place in the city."

"Well, we don't have to," Greg amended. "But a lot of my clients are in the city, so it makes life easier for me to live there."

"What sort of work do you do?"

"I'm a financial consultant. Actually, I was out here this weekend working with Wilbur Lately," Greg said.

"Oh. I'm so sorry. Were you close friends?" I asked.

"Yes, we were. We'd been working together for years and we'd become friends over that time. That's how Cinda and I learned about Galena."

"How did you and Wilbur meet?"

"Wilbur was looking for a financial planner before he retired. A mutual friend referred him to me. I'd been representing Alan for years and Alan and Wilbur worked together at Chicago Engineering. This past year Wilbur and I had been working on his trust."

"Wilbur had a trust?"

"Yes, actually, that's one of the things I wanted to tell you about. Johnny told me he'd called you and asked for your help. So, I wouldn't normally talk about a client's affairs but in this case, I thought you should know about this sooner rather than later."

"Know what?" I asked. He had my attention now.

"Well, I don't know how this plays into what happened to

Wilbur, but we'd been talking to JDCF, you know, the Jo Daviess Conservation Foundation, about selling them Wilbur's land. In fact, we were ready to close the deal at one point but Montey Foot, JDCF's financial consultant, kept delaying. I thought that was really odd because I know the JDCF Board was very interested in acquiring Wilbur's land. They'd just bought some adjacent land last year and their goal is to preserve larger tracts of land. The wildlife need undivided acreage to really thrive. But I'm digressing. What I wanted to tell you is, I really got to wondering why Montey kept delaying the deal so I made a few discreet inquiries. What I found out, from a friend of mine in the Attorney General's office, is that the SEC is investigating Montey Foot."

"For what? Do you think this has something to do with Wilbur's death?"

"I don't know. But I can tell you that they're investigating Montey for fraud. They think he was running a Ponzi scheme—you know, using money from clients' funds to pay returns to other investors. That pyramid scheme can only work so long and then you run out of new clients to give you money. Or, one of your clients wants a big chunk of their money back, which is what happened with JDCF. JDCF planned to pull $5,000,000 in cash out of Montey's investment fund."

"Wow! I didn't realize the land was worth that much," I said.

"Wilbur had 833 acres and at $6,000 per acre, that's what it comes to. I don't think Montey had that much money in JDCF's account even though the statements he sent to JDCF said he did. I think that's why Montey kept putting off the closing. I have it on good authority that they're doing an audit of Montey's records and accounts right now. I think they'll be announcing an arrest within days," Greg said.

"But I still don't see how killing Wilbur helped Montey," I said.

"Unless Montey figured that would put the closing off permanently," Cinda said.

"Greg, did Montey know you were on to him?" I asked.

"I expect he did," Greg said.

"Do you think he could have meant that bronze statue to hit you?" I asked. "I mean, maybe he thought you were stirring up trouble for him and he wanted to make you stop," I said.

"My heavens!" Cinda gasped and grabbed Greg's arm. Truffs went on high alert.

"I hadn't thought of that!" Greg said. "But I suppose it's possible. I was standing next to Wilbur at the gallery. We were talking about the trust he'd just set up," Greg said.

"You mentioned the trust before. How does that fit in?" I asked.

"Well, after Montey had been putting off the closing for so long, Wilbur and I started talking about alternatives. And we came up with the idea of a life trust. Wilbur had just secretly put all his real estate into a trust for his own benefit during his lifetime and then Johnny's."

"Oh no!" I said.

Cinda and Greg looked at me in surprise. "What's wrong?" Greg asked.

"Detective Cavanaugh will think Johnny killed Wilbur for sure when he learns about the trust! Don't you see? If Johnny gets the trust after Wilbur's death, then that gives Johnny motive to kill Wilbur so he'd come into control of Wilbur's land and could go ahead with the real estate development he was working on with Bull Skittles."

"No, No. It wouldn't work that way. You see, under the terms of the trust, Johnny can't sell or develop the property until he's 50 years old."

"What! So Bull Skittles' development project can't go forward?"

"Nope. At least not on Wilbur's land it can't. Not until Johnny reaches 50. And that's about 20 years away. Wilbur's idea was if Johnny managed the farm for the next 20 years, he'd come to love the property as much as Wilbur does—did. If Johnny still wanted to sell the property then, well, he'd be free to do it. It wasn't like there was any other family to pass the land along to. Johnny was it," Greg said. "Wilbur felt that at 50 Johnny would be mature enough to make a decision he wouldn't regret later."

"You mean a decision like developing the property?"

"Precisely," Greg responded.

"So, I guess that lets Bull Skittles off the hook, too. I mean, if he had a motive it would have been to get Wilbur out of the way so Johnny could inherit the land and go on with the development," I said.

"Well, not really," Greg said. "You see, Wilbur hadn't told anyone else about the trust yet. Not even Johnny knew. So

Bull could still have been trying to prevent Wilbur from selling his land to JDCF," Greg said.

"And so could Johnny," I thought to myself.

"But there's more," Greg said.

"More!"

"Yes. Yesterday, I was getting together information from Wilbur's computer files for his estate. Johnny's the executor and he asked me to help him with the probate. I know it's soon to be doing this, but I needed to get a few bits of information to get started. Anyway, I came across a file that had a bunch of letters, threatening letters, from a guy named Ron Reilley. I think he could be your murderer. I've never seen such anger in writing!" Greg said.

"Great. I mean, great that you've found a suspect other than Johnny. Did you tell Detective Cavanaugh?"

"I did. I made copies and gave them to him. They're tracking down Ron Reilley now. From what I hear, he's actually in Galena. Detective Cavanaugh said he'd traced Reilley's credit card and they show he's been staying at a cabin not far from here. I think he said it was the llama place on Blackjack Road. Does that mean anything to you?"

"Yes! There's a log cabin rental place about five miles from here, closer to town. They raise alpaca though, not llamas."

"Alpaca, llamas, what's the difference?"

"Well, if you're asking literally, they're very different animals. Alpaca's are calmer and they have much finer wool.

Llamas will spit at you if you get them riled up. Anyway, if Ron Reilley was staying there Friday he could easily have been at the gallery. It was an invitation only opening, but no one would have stopped him at the door. He could have been following Wilbur and just taken the opportunity to get his revenge," I postulated.

"I hate to think of anyone being so angry," Cinda said.

"But at least it gives Detective Cavanaugh someone other than Johnny to pursue as a suspect," I said.

Chapter Eight

Brothers and Sisters

Monday Afternoon

After Greg and Cinda left, about 11:00 a.m., I decided to check on my new orchid greenhouse. For several years I'd kept my burgeoning orchid collection in my home. But last month, I had a modest greenhouse constructed and I find myself puttering around in there anytime I get a chance. The greenhouse is located on the east side of my home. It's attached by a breezeway, a sort of open sided walkway with a roof, leading to the glass and metal structure. The greenhouse is 50 feet long and 30 feet wide, with three rows of slotted wooden shelves. There are also poles running lengthwise about seven feet off the floor to hold hanging orchids. So, between those poles and the shelves, I can accommodate about 150 orchids. That leaves me lots of room for collecting more orchid plants—yea!

I staked a few spikes, which sounds rather industrial but it really isn't. Orchids bloom on a sort of branch they shoot out called a spike. My phalaenopsis orchids spike twice a year, usually in February and October, with the winter blooms being the most prolific. It's always a treat in the cold, gray Midwest winter to see flowers in bloom. It makes the care of the plants the other ten months of the year worth the effort.

Several orchids were having *kikis,* which is the Hawaiian word for babies. The *kikis* look like miniature orchid plants and they grow directly from the spike after the orchid has stopped blooming. The best procedure is to let the *kiki* grow attached to its mother plant until it has formed air roots of its own. When the *kiki's* air roots are about four inches long, the *kiki* will be able to sustain itself. Then, with a sterilized razor blade, you cut the spike about one inch below the *kiki.* Next, you plant the *kiki* in a three inch plastic pot filled with an orchid potting mix made up of equal parts: pine bark, sphagnum moss and perlite. Then you have another orchid plant.

Although there are a few terrestrial orchids, most orchids do not grow in soil. In fact, potting an orchid in soil would eventually kill the orchid by keeping its roots too wet and causing them to rot. The goal in watering orchids is to give them enough water to feed them and then to let them dry out just before you water them again. That keeps their roots healthy. So every few years, as the bark mix degrades and composts itself into soil, you should repot your orchids into fresh bark mix.

An hour flew by as I puttered with my plants. When I was finished with the orchids, I texted Marsha and Bella and reminded them that bathing suits and cover-ups were *de rigueur* on St. Barths and to pack very lightly in one small carry-on each. I also asked them to pass the word along to Ed and Destiny, respectively. That done, I decided to check on Ken and Tony to see how their goat project was coming along.

I hopped on the ATV and headed out to the six acre tract of land we'd agreed would serve as our goat farm. My property has five ridges that had been cleared and planted in corn many years back. When I bought the property, I took it out of corn and planted it in prairie grasses and wildflowers. The soil had been pretty well eroded from the corn farming, but there was enough left to support a good prairie. And each year the plants build up more soil as the prior year's grasses and leaves decompose and the plants' roots form a strong web of support for the soil. Now, six years into my prairie restoration, I had acres of five foot tall grasses interspersed with thousands of wildflowers. The prairie is a constantly changing palette of color from spring through the fall. The goats would probably keep the plant growth down on their six acres, but they'd add their own level of interest to country life.

I found Ken and Tony in the pole barn, just finishing their milking stand construction project. They had our solid black doe, Juliet, between them and were leading her into the stand. She had other ideas and wasn't at all sure she wanted to go there. I had to laugh at the sight of them. Ken thought offering her a favorite feed might work. He grabbed some blackberry branches he'd collected for the goats and offered Juliet a bite. She took the branch and chomped down happily.

Ken dangled another branch in front of her and then moved toward the stand. Juliet followed and in a few more steps he had her on the stand.

"Hey, good work!" I said. "Now let's see you milk her!"

Ken gave me a look, then he and Tony exchanged glances.

"Go ahead," Tony said. "I'll have plenty of opportunities. They have to be milked every day, you know, and I'll be the one here to do it," Tony said.

Ken gave Juliet the rest of the branches and grabbed a stool. He sat down alongside Juliet and put the milk pail under her udder. He reached over and gingerly grasped her teat and gently pulled. Milk squirted out, some of which even went into the bucket.

"Great work!" I said, laughing.

"Juliet's doing the main work. I'm just assisting here," Ken said, with a laugh as well. Juliet didn't seem to mind the process. She continued chewing her blackberry branches giving an occasional glance back at Ken.

When the milking demonstration was over, Ken and Tony showed me the sleeping platforms they'd constructed the other day for the goats. "We figured we'd make five of these," Tony said. Each platform was like a little wooden deck, raised up about a foot off the ground. They were about ten feet long by six feet wide.

"That should accommodate the herd. We'll build more as we get more goats," Ken said.

"More goats?" I asked.

"Well, we have twelve does and they'll each have one to three kids a year. So, yup, I'd say we'll be having more goats," Ken said.

"Are you up for all the milking?" I asked Tony.

"Well, I figure I'll start out being the milker and then, when the goat cheese money comes rolling in, we might hire more staff," Tony said.

"Tony and Louise are coming in on the Galena Goat Cheese Venture," Ken said. "We figure there'll be the five of us: you provide the goats, land and housing, Tony and Louise will do the feeding and milking, I'll make the goat cheese, and Bella will sell it. We've already got all of our labor and our fixed costs covered, so it should be fun and profitable."

"People love goat cheese. And with Bella's catering business and her shop, we should have demand and distribution covered," Tony said.

"I'm impressed. You guys have really given this some thought," I said.

I couldn't take my eyes off the little kids. They were as cute as puppy dogs. They had the softest fur and fuzzy ears and they seemed to love being petted. We'd named them all after characters in Shakespeare's plays, a reminder of Ken's days as an English professor.

"Now, the question is, can you recognize them all?" I asked Ken.

He got up from his milking stool and said, "Of course! I spent all morning with them. Besides Juliet here, we have our buck, Romeo; and our three little wethers: Macbeth, Othello, and Henry," Ken said walking over to the three male kids. "Come on, the other does are outside," Ken said. The three of us left the open barn and walked out into the field. Ken moved into the center of the little herd and pointed to each of the goats as he said: "Lady M, Dessie (short for Desdemona), Kate (short for Katherine), Anne, Beatrice, Gertie (short for Gertrude) Hermia, Helena, Rosalind, Celia and Titania. How'd I do?"

"Bravo! I think you and Tony both deserve some lunch! I've got some great dishes from Bella's we can have."

"Sound's wonderful," Ken said.

"It does sound great and I'm sorry I can't join you. Louise and I have plans for the afternoon. You two go ahead. I'll just finish up here and see you tomorrow," Tony said.

"Say hello to Louise for me. Tell her I'll call her later with our travel info for Wednesday," I said. Louise and Tony have become like family to me over the past few years. Thanks to them I'm able to walk out the door when I travel without worrying about Truffs, my orchids, the house or, now, the goats. Tony and Louise take care of them all.

Ken and I raced back to the house on our ATV's. These four wheeled all terrain vehicles are a great way to get around the property if you're in a hurry, or even if you aren't. They're much more stable than the old three wheel design and you can use them to carry all sorts of things, from painting supplies to bags of bird seed.

Over lunch, Ken and I got to talking about Wilbur. I filled

him in on Greg's discovery about Montey's pyramid scheme and Wilbur's trust. "So, let's make a list of suspects," I said.

"Well, besides Detective Cavanaugh's first choice of Johnny, I guess we can put Bull Skittles on the list, since he'll lose a bundle if the development project doesn't go forward," Ken said.

"Which, I suppose, it won't now that the property's in a trust that prevents development for the next 20 years," I said.

"But, Bull Skittles doesn't know that, and he might have been trying to speed up Johnny's inheriting the land so he and Johnny could develop it," Ken said.

"Right. And then we have Montey, who might have been trying to kill Greg when he was standing next to Wilbur and stop him from looking into the Ponzi scheme he was running," I said.

"Or Montey might have been trying to squash the JDCF deal by killing Wilbur," Ken said. "And Destiny thinks there's a ghost that's responsible," Ken added.

"I don't think we'd convince Detective Cavanaugh that a ghost did it. Let's just try to see if we can find someone in the here and now," I said.

"And what about Isolde?" Ken asked. "What does she gain if Wilbur's gone?"

"I think she had more to lose," I said. "After all, Wilbur ran the company she worked for. I thought for a minute and then said, "You're right, though. We don't really know what happens to Prairie Fuels now that Wilbur's gone. Isolde said she'd have a patent shortly. Maybe she and Wilbur fought about that. Maybe he thought it was his."

"But then why did someone rifle through Wilbur's files? How does that fit in?" Ken asked.

"I don't know. Maybe we should go look at Wilbur's office. That might give us some ideas," I said. "And don't forget Zay Lately. Maybe she killed her 'ex.' We know she had a grudge against the gallery. Maybe the gallery was the real target," I suggested.

"And don't forget Ron Reilley. We shouldn't ignore the obvious. He's the one who had it in for Wilbur. He has the motive and now we know he was in Galena on Friday, so he had the opportunity," Ken said.

"Good point. Let's google him and see what we can find out on the computer," I said.

We went into my office and I woke up my laptop. It whirred to life and the screen lit up revealing one of my favorite Jan Van Huysum paintings that I use as a screen saver. I opened my browser window and googled Ronald Reilley.

We found a White Page entry that listed a phone and PO Box address in Chicago. I also got a hit on a court record and, with a little research, found that Ron Reilley had been involved in a personal injury suit about three years ago. He'd been the plaintiff and it looked like he'd gotten a pretty good settlement. I jotted down the address and the case number in my little spiral notebook. 'Reilley' was an unusual spelling; most people spelled it 'Reilly'. So I was pretty sure I had the right Ron Reilley. I expanded the search and found a Jan Reilley in Elizabeth, just 15 miles from here. I decided to give her a call just to see if by any chance she knew Ron Reilley.

Jan answered the phone on the third ring.

"Is this Jan Reilley?" I asked.

"Yes, who's calling?" she asked.

"This is Karen Prince. I'm looking for Ron Reilley. I was wondering if by any chance you were related to him and could tell me where I might find him," I said, being as courteous and disarming as I could.

There was dead silence on the other end of the line.

"Jan, nothing's wrong. I just want to ask Ron a few questions about his work with Wilbur Lately," I added with the hope that this would help Jan feel comfortable in talking to me.

More silence. Then she said, "What is this about?"

When she said that, I realized she definitely knew Ron or she wouldn't have been asking me that.

"As I said, it's about his work at Chicago Engineering."

"I don't understand. Why are you calling now? My brother disappeared last year," Jan said.

Now it was my turn to be silent. But I recovered and said, "I'm so sorry. I didn't know. Maybe we have the wrong Ron Reilley," I suggested.

"I don't think there are two Ron Reilley's that worked at Chicago Engineering with Wilbur Lately," Jan said.

I was confused. Hadn't someone just told me that Ron

Reilley was staying at the Alpaca Ranch? Hadn't Greg just found letters from Ron Reilley threatening Wilbur? Was Jan trying to protect her brother by pretending she didn't know where he was? What was going on here?

"I'm sorry. I was told your brother had been writing to Wilbur recently. Apparently there'd been some animosity between them relating back to their work at Chicago Engineering," I said. "Were you aware of that?" I asked.

"I know Wilbur fired Ron, if that's what you mean," Jan said.

"Yes, that's what I'd heard. I'm so sorry to disturb you. But could I ask you one more question?"

She paused, then said, "All right."

"I saw somewhere that your brother was in a car accident a few years ago and that he'd gotten a settlement from the driver that hit him. Is that right?" I asked.

She paused and then said, "Yes, Ron was hit by a drunk driver just after he was fired. The defendant was quite wealthy and settled the case with an agreement to pay Ron $4,000 per month for life," Jan said.

"Is Ron still collecting that? I asked.

"I don't know. As I said, Ron just disappeared. It's not that we saw a lot of each other, but he'd call every now and then and keep in touch. I've tried to reach him but his number's been disconnected and I haven't heard from him in almost a year. I don't have any way of getting in touch with him," Jan said. I could hear the tears welling up in her throat.

I believed she really hadn't seen him.

"Thank you, Jan. I'm sorry to have troubled you. I appreciate your taking the time to talk to me," I said.

"Sure. If you find out anything about my brother, would you let me know?"

"Of course," I said and we hung up.

Ken had been listening in on the extension—sneaky, but better than my trying to recap everything for him.

"This is getting curiouser and curiouser," Ken said.

"Let's see what Isolde knows about this," I said to Ken.

We gave Isolde a call and, together, filled her in on what we'd found out about Ron Reilley: his injury, his settlement award, his disappearance, the threatening letters Greg had found, and the fact that Detective Cavanaugh had tracked down Ron Reilley staying at the Alpaca Ranch outside Galena.

"I don't understand," Isolde said. "Let me talk to some friends from Chicago Engineering and get back to you."

When we hung up with Isolde, I put in a call to Detective Cavanaugh to tell him what we'd learned. I'd been putting off talking to him because he'd specifically asked me to leave the investigation to him. But this information was too weird to sit on. I had to call. Unfortunately, I got his voice mail, so I left a message with everything we'd learned and asked him to get back to me. That was the best that I could do.

By now it was nearly 3:00 p.m., and Ken had to get back home to Baxter. He hadn't brought the big fellow with him because he wasn't sure how Baxter would take to the goats and vice versa. We figured it was better to leave that introduction for another day, after the goats were accustomed to their new home. Then again, maybe there was really no need to make the introduction at all.

"Talk to you tomorrow," I said, giving Ken a kiss as he headed out the door.

Chapter Nine

Getting Stuck

Tuesday

Isolde called early Tuesday morning and said she had found some information on Ron Reilley that she wanted to show us. She asked if Ken and I would meet her at her place. I said we would and immediately began wondering what Isolde had found out and how that would fit with Ron's sister's story. Ron's disappearing and then being at the Alpaca Ranch was odd. Could his sister have been lying? And if she was, the question was why would she? Maybe Ron wanted to keep a low profile and told his sister to tell everyone he'd disappeared. That'd be pretty weird in itself. It was sure looking like Ron could be our guy, especially if he was in hiding. Maybe that was his plan to get away with murder—to pretend to be missing, or even dead, and then kill Wilbur.

I wanted to find out everything I could about Ron Reilley and get that information over to Detective Cavanaugh. I was feeling pretty guilty about leaving for St. Barths on Wednesday with Johnny still the prime suspect. But I knew Ken was right. Everyone I'd invited was really looking forward to this trip so I couldn't just cancel it. Still, I'd sure feel better if I could turn up some leads for Detective Cavanaugh to look into while we were gone, preferably something that led away from Johnny.

Ken and I had agreed to meet at Isolde's because I'd planned to stop and do some shopping on the way home, not one of his favorite activities.

I took Blackjack Road to Highway 20, and then turned right onto Highway 20 heading away from Galena. A few miles outside of town, Highway 20 sweeps around a wide curve offering a view of Galena's red brick buildings and five white church steeples in the distance, all surrounded by miles and miles of rolling farmland as far as the eye can see. This bit of road is called Horseshoe Bend. The view takes your breath away—in part because it's so beautiful and in part because you're driving at highway speeds with a sharp upslope on one side of you and a sheer drop-off on the other. You can't help but be torn between keeping your eyes on the road and taking in that dramatic view. I found myself holding my breath as I rounded the curve and coasted down the steep incline. The road descended until it was level with the surrounding farm fields.

I left Highway 20 at the next crossing, turning left onto Horseshoe Mound Road. Isolde said she lived on this road, just down from Johnny and Wilbur. I knew my way to their place from the time Johnny and I did some outdoor landscape painting there last October. Galena's fall color is more than memorable and painting the scenery is a great way to really take it all in.

Horseshoe Mound Road is seal coated so my low slung Boxster did all right on it. With only four inches of clearance, I assiduously avoid seriously rutted roads like River Road or Devil's Ladder with my little sports car.

In a few miles, I drove by Johnny and Wilbur's white farm house on my left. I checked my odometer and continued precisely two more miles as Isolde had directed. There it was. A two-story red brick home with four red brick pillars, just as she'd described. Ken's truck was in the driveway and I parked next to it. As I got out, Baxter recognized me and pranced back and forth in the bed of the pickup. He gave a huge bark and wagged his tail like crazy.

"Hey boy!" I said. "What are you doing out here?"

My talking to him didn't do anything to calm Baxter down. His barking took on a new level of energy.

"No, sorry. I can't come up there. I have to go into the house. But we'll be out in a little bit and we'll visit then, all right?" I said.

Baxter settled down when he realized I wasn't staying out there with him. He was settling back down on his bedding as I walked up the porch steps.

As I raised my hand to knock, I was startled to have the front door swing open. Isolde stood there with a wooden smile on her face.

"Karen. So glad you could make it on such short notice," Isolde said. "Come in. Ken is already here, as you saw."

I followed Isolde into the living room and Ken stood up to greet me. Standing behind Isolde, Ken raised his eyebrows and tilted his head. I wasn't quite sure what he was trying to tell me. It sort of seemed he was nodding toward the door like he wanted to go, but we'd just gotten there, so that didn't make sense. And besides, I wanted to hear what she had to say about Ron Reilley.

"Come into the kitchen while I put some coffee on for us, won't you?" Isolde said to the two of us.

I followed Isolde and Ken followed me down the dark hallway leading to the kitchen.

"Have a seat at the table, please. I'd rather talk in here, if you don't mind being informal," Isolde said.

"Not at all," I said and pulled out one of the old oak chairs around the kitchen table.

Ken took a seat across from me. When I went to scoot myself in closer to the table something felt wrong. I tried to shift my weight and realized, to put it delicately, that my skirt was stuck to the chair seat.

I looked over at Ken and he was in the same predicament. "Don't touch the chair seat with your hands," Ken whispered to me.

"What's going on here?" I exclaimed as I looked over at Isolde. She stood in front of the kitchen range. She was holding something metal but it sure wasn't a coffeepot.

"She has a gun!" I said and flung myself, chair and all, to the floor then slid under the table.

"That's not going to help you. Both of you stay right where you are," Isolde commanded.

Keeping the gun pointed at us with one hand, Isolde grabbed a larger gun in the other. She came toward the table and I realized that the second gun she'd picked up was some sort of dispensing gun.

"Don't move," Isolde said as she approached the table. She held the real gun at Ken's head and squirted something from the dispensing gun onto the floor around the legs of Ken's chair.

"That's good. Let me get the bottom of those chair legs. That's right," she said. From my worm's eye vantage point I could see that she was gluing Ken's chair to the floor with him in it!

"Isolde, what the heck are you doing? Are you in this with Ron Reilley? Did you kill Wilbur? Why? Why are you doing this?" I rapid fired questions at her. Words were all I had right now and I wanted to know what was going on.

Isolde moved over to my side of the table now and she seemed to be considering whether to glue me to the floor on my side under the table or somehow get my chair upright to match Ken's. She went for symmetry. She held the gun at my head now and directed me to get up. That's not as easy to do with a chair glued to your skirt as you might think.

I wiggled around on the floor stalling for time.

"Come on, come on. Get up," she commanded.

My mind was racing thinking of how to get out of this. Ken was shifting in his chair trying to get some leverage to snap the chair seat off its legs. I stalled and said, with as much authority as I could muster, "I'll get up but, first, tell me why you're doing this!"

Isolde looked at me with surprise. Then she said, "Feisty, huh? Well, I suppose it won't hurt to tell you now. You won't be around much longer to share the story, unfortunately for you."

"You're going to shoot us?" I asked.

"Not unless you do something stupid to make me," Isolde said. "No, you're going to go *Ka-boom*!" She exploded the last word.

Ken and I looked at each other. We had to do something! This lady was definitely nuts. And, unfortunately, she had a gun—never a good combination.

"Now get going and scoot your chair out from under that table!" Isolde demanded.

At this point, I didn't have much choice. Somehow I made it to my feet in a sort of crouch position. The chair added considerable weight to my behind. I thought about running in this crouched position with the chair dangling from me and almost laughed. Then I considered swinging around quickly and knocking Isolde off her feet with the chair legs. But she was holding the gun and I didn't think I should risk her firing it. The impact itself might make her pull the trigger.

Isolde came over and gave me a shove backward. My

chair's legs hit the floor and I rocked forward to offset the backward momentum. My chair teetered but somehow I was able to stay upright. Then she glued my chair legs to the floor the same way she had Ken's.

"What good will killing us do?" Ken asked.

"Why, they'll find you here. What's left of you, anyway. And they'll find Ron Reilley," she said.

Ken and I looked at each other. "I thought Ron Reilley disappeared a year ago," Ken said.

"That's enough with the questions. That's what got you into this position. If you hadn't been asking so many questions about Ron Reilley, I wouldn't have to kill you," Isolde said.

She gave my chair another shove to see if it would move. Unfortunately, it didn't.

"What do you have in that glue gun?" I asked. I was astounded that anything could cause two surfaces to adhere so quickly and so firmly.

"It's a little something I cooked up in the lab," she cackled. "I should probably patent this as well. But I'll have all the money I need from the Miscanthus patent. I couldn't let Wilbur take all the credit for that, you know."

"Is that what all this is about? A patent?"

"Don't sound so shocked. That patent is very valuable. My attorney tells me I'll be able to license it for millions," Isolde said.

"OK. But, again, why kill us?" Ken asked.

"Because you've been poking your nose where it doesn't belong. You were looking into Ron Reilley's settlement payments. I couldn't let you track those back to us," Isolde said.

"Who is 'us'?" I asked.

"Never you mind," Isolde said. "Now you two stay put!"

Isolde walked over to the closed pantry and opened the doors. We could hear her huffing and grunting. She came back into our sight dragging an unconscious man.

Chapter Ten

Kaboom

Still Tuesday Afternoon

"Is that Ron Reilley?" Ken asked.

"That's him," Isolde said. She was short of breath from dragging him but she still had her gun—the real one. "So you see now, you two should have left things alone. You could have lived. But now, now, I'm afraid it's too late for that," Isolde said.

She lifted up a large pot that had been sitting, upside down, in the middle of the table. Now we could see a black box with a red digital display blinking: 10:00, then 9:59, then 9:58. It was a time bomb!

"So you can see why I have to leave," Isolde laughed

maniacally and then ran out the back door.

"Maybe I can rock around enough to break the chair legs," Ken said, gasping. But he was limited by the chair legs being glued in place.

We heard Isolde's car start and drive away.

Ken called out "Baxter. Here boy. Baxter," at the top of his lungs. Then he let out a piercing whistle that rivaled the doorman's taxi whistle at my old Chicago condo. And that was saying a lot.

"I didn't know you could do that!"

"Lots of things you don't know about me yet," Ken said.

"Well, I'd like a little more time to learn about them. Let's figure out how we're getting out of here!" I said.

Then it struck me. My back wasn't glued to the chair, just my denim skirt. I unzipped my skirt and slipped out of it being extremely careful not to touch the chair.

"Great! Grab a knife and cut me out of these jeans," Ken said. "I don't think I bend in ways that would let me get out of them while they're still glued down like this!"

Now Baxter was at the kitchen door barking like crazy. If there'd been any neighbors nearby they might have come over to see what the ruckus was. But we were in the country and there weren't any neighbors near enough to hear Baxter or us. Anyway, we were at 8:58 and counting down!

I pulled open drawers and found a cutlery knife. "Careful!" Ken said as I slid the knife between the fabric and his waistband.

In a few minutes Ken was free, too. We grabbed Ron Reilly, or whomever he was, and pulled him out of the kitchen. We had a job of it keeping Baxter from going into the kitchen while we were dragging Reilley out.

Finally outside, we propped Reilley between the two of us with his arms draped over our shoulders. We sort of walked/dragged him away from the house and into the back seat of Ken's truck.

Baxter followed us and hopped in the front passenger seat of the truck. Quickly, I got into the Boxster and started it up. We were both just out of the driveway when the house went:
Ka-boom!

Chapter Eleven

Petal to the Metal

Tuesday Afternoon

Ken was in his truck, pantless, with a drugged man propped in the back seat. Baxter, his ever faithful dog, was in the front seat with Ken. I was in my sports car, skirtless, wishing I'd taken time to put up the convertible top earlier when I'd parked. We were driving down Horseshoe Mound Road heading toward Highway 20. What to do? We had to get Ron Reilley to a hospital. We had to find Isolde—or at least someone did. That sounded like a job for Detective Cavanaugh. In all the commotion getting out of Isolde's house, we hadn't coordinated any sort of plan—other than getting the heck out of there before the blast!

My mind raced, searching for solutions. The sound of

frogs startled me. It was my cell phone. I hadn't even re-alized I'd had my purse draped over my shoulder this whole time! Ken usually kept his cell phone in his truck. At least we could talk to each other! I answered my phone and heard Ken's voice: "You all right?"

"Yes. You?"

"I'm okay but Reilley here is starting to come to. Can you call Cavanaugh and have him meet us at the Emergency Room? We could try to take this guy into the hospital ourselves but, when he comes to, he might have other ideas. And chasing him around the way we're dressed probably wouldn't work out all that well," Ken said.

"Right. I'll see you at Galena Hospital, then. I'll try to stay behind you, but if we get separated I'll see you at the Emer-gency Room entrance," I said and rang off.

I dialed Detective Cavanaugh's office and this time he picked up.

"Detective Cavanaugh, it's Karen Prince. I have an emer-gency and need your help. Two emergencies, actually. Can you meet Ken and me at the Galena Hospital ER right away? We're on our way there with Ron Reilley. He's been drugged and he needs medical attention. I don't know what Isolde gave him, but Ken says he's starting to come out of it. He might get violent if he thinks we're the ones who drugged him," I said.

"Slow down. Slow down. I've got Ron Reilley in my custody. He's in lock up right now," Detective Cavanaugh said.

"What! Detective Cavanaugh, I don't understand. Isolde tried to kill Ken and me. That I know for sure. And she had another man there. He was drugged. She tried to kill all three of us! She blew up her house and she meant for the three of us to be in it when it exploded. We got out just in time!" I said. "You have to have her arrested now!"

"You're not making a lot of sense," Detective Cavanaugh said.

"Trust me on this. With all we've been through, please just trust me and do two things: meet us at the ER entrance right away and have someone find and arrest Isolde. I'll give you all the details at the ER," I said.

Detective Cavanaugh paused. He took a breath and said, "We just got the report on the explosion. The fire department's been called and they're on their way there now. Is there anyone else in the house?"

"No, we all got out. Does this mean you'll meet us at the ER?"

"I'll be there in five minutes," Detective Cavanaugh said. "And I'll let the fire department know they don't have to go into the house for a search and rescue. Thank you. Where are you, Karen?" Detective Cavanaugh asked.

"We're on Highway 20 now, just going over the bridge before town," I said.

"I should get to the hospital the same time you do. Stay in the car with that guy if you get there first," Detective Cavanaugh said.

"Oh, we will!" I said. "Detective, one more thing. Do you have any spare clothes there?"

"What?"

"Never mind. I have an idea. See you in five minutes," I said and rang off.

I thought about calling the ER and asking for gowns to be brought out to our cars but, of course, they'd think I was crazy. Then I remembered the emergency blankets I kept in the boot of the Boxster. It would look weird but better than the alternative.

I stayed on Ken's tail. There are six lights in Galena and somehow we made them all green. As we pulled into the new hospital's parking area I saw Detective Cavanaugh's white squad car over by the ER entrance. Ken was driving over to him but I stopped at a remote corner of the lot and pulled the latch by the side of my seat to pop open the front hood. I opened the door and scurried out to grab the two blankets as fast as I could. I wrapped one around my waist to make an impromptu skirt, then hopped back into the car and drove over to the ER entrance, pulling in right behind Ken. I grabbed the other blanket and hurried over to Ken's side of the truck. Detective Cavanaugh was just getting out of his vehicle when I passed the blanket to Ken through the driver's side window. I peered into the truck and noticed that Ron Reilley Number Two was shifting in his seat. At least he was still alive.

Detective Cavanaugh came up beside me and looked at my homemade blanket-skirt. "I'll give you the full story inside, but basically, Isolde told us this guy was Ron Reilley. She had us all trapped in her kitchen with a bomb set to go off. We managed to get out of there but not with all of our clothes," I said. "Right now we'd better get this guy into the hospital!"

Detective Cavanaugh went around to the passenger's side door. Ron Reilley was still leaning against the back seat window, semi-conscious. Baxter gave a huge bark at the sight of Detective Cavanaugh looking in the window.

"Ken, can you get out and help me with this guy? And can you keep your dog in the truck?" Detective Cavanaugh asked. Baxter was imposing, even to someone Detective Cavanaugh's size.

Detective Cavanaugh looked in the truck window and saw Ken's bare legs sticking out beneath the blanket in his lap. "It's a long story," Ken said, and scooted out of the truck, turning his blanket into a kilt.

"Any skort in a storm," Ken said and we both broke out laughing and hugged each other.

"What's a skort?" Detective Cavanaugh asked.

We both looked at him. "It's a kind of a skirt," I said and giggled again. The combination of adrenaline and relief was making us giddy.

Ken put his hands on my shoulders and staring into my eyes said, "You never looked so good!" He gave me that great grin of his then a serious kiss.

"Could you two break it up over there and give me a hand?" Detective Cavanaugh shouted.

Baxter barked again. He seemed to share our joy at still being alive.

As Ken helped Detective Cavanaugh get Reilley out of the truck, I went into the ER lobby to get a wheelchair. When we rolled our guy in, Detective Cavanaugh's presence cut through the usual administrative red tape and we were directed back to a sheeted cubicle.

The ER doctor listened to Ron Reilley's heart then told us, "He'll be all right. I think he's taken some sleeping pills but his vitals are strong. He'll come out of this soon. I'll order some follow-up blood work. Is this man in your custody?" the doctor asked Detective Cavanaugh.

"I'm holding him for questioning. I'll have a guard stationed with him if that's all right with you. I need to talk to him when he comes to. In the meantime, I'll run his prints. I have a kit in the squad car," Detective Cavanaugh said.

A few minutes later, as Detective Cavanaugh was taking Ron Reilley Number Two's fingerprints, Ken and I gave Cavanaugh the blow by blow recap of our narrow escape.

We had just finished with our tale when Detective Cavanaugh's phone rang. His officers had taken Isolde into custody. She'd gone to the bank and grocery store, running errands as if nothing had happened. Once she realized her plan had failed and that we were alive and well, she confessed to everything.

"Her plan had been to pretend she had just gone out for the day and to come back and find her home on fire. She figured the police would find the two of you and Ron Reilley Number Two there—dead. People would have blamed Ron Reilley for your deaths as well as Wilbur's and his own," Detective Cavanaugh said.

I jumped in, "So, Isolde figured she'd get off scot-free. She'd lose her house, but that was a price she was willing to pay for her alibi. And she'd probably get insurance money to cover that. And eventually she'd have the licensing fees from her patent."

"But now, your testimony will put her behind bars for a very long time. And the insurance company won't pay her a cent because she set the bomb herself," Detective Cavanaugh said.

"But what about the guy you have in jail? Is he the real Ron Reilley? And if he is, who's in this hospital bed?" I asked.

Chapter Twelve

Will the Real Ron Reilley Please Stand Up?

Still Tuesday

"The prints came back on Ron Reilley Number One," Detective Cavanaugh said. "His real name is Sol Sneed. He's a con artist and he's been passing himself off as Ron Reilley around town here. He had the real Ron Reilley's credit card and driver's license in his wallet. Apparently, he and Isolde had been holding the real Ron Reilley captive for quite a while."

"Did Sol Sneed kill Wilbur?" Ken asked.

"No. That was Isolde. She dropped that bronze on Wilbur. But Sol and Isolde were partners in this whole scheme, so he's an accessory to Wilbur's murder and Reilley's kidnapping and false imprisonment," Detective Cavanaugh said.

"So that's why Ron Reilley didn't call his sister. He couldn't!" I said. I told Detective Cavanaugh about my conversation with Jan Reilley.

"I followed up on the real Ron Reilley's lawsuit and learned that the fellow who hit him was still making the settlement payments each month," Detective Cavanaugh said. "And the checks were being cashed regularly."

"So Sol pretended to be Ron Reilley for the past year to collect the payments!" I said.

"Yes. They planned to blame Ron Reilley for Wilbur's murder. Isolde would get the patent and all the patent fees. And with Ron Reilley dead, Sol would go back to being Sol," Detective Cavanaugh said.

"I'll bet that patent doesn't even really belong to Isolde," I said. "I think that's why she killed Wilbur in the first place. Think about it. Johnny told me that someone had gone through Wilbur's files. He said Isolde had gotten to the office just before he had and found the break-in. I'll bet she'd really been there for quite a while. She must have been looking for Wilbur's copy of their agreement. I think she wanted to destroy anything that showed that Wilbur or his company had any right to the patent. Even after Wilbur was dead, she was probably afraid that Johnny might find the real agreement in his Uncle's papers and sue her to take the patent rights away from her," I said.

"So the patent really belongs to Wilbur's Estate. And Johnny's the sole beneficiary, so Johnny will inherit the patent," Ken said.

"I'd better call Johnny and tell him the news about Isolde and Sol and the patent," I said.

"He'll be relieved to know he's not a suspect anymore," Ken said.

"And he's about to become very wealthy with those patent rights," I said.

Chapter Thirteen

Plane Talk

Wednesday

Wednesday was our travel day. I arrived at the airstrip at 6:45 a.m. Our captain, Burt Castle, was already there going over the plane and doing his preflight inspection.

"Hi Burt! You ready for a week in the Caribbean?" I asked.

"Sure am," he said.

I looked at the plane and did a double take. "This isn't the same plane you flew to Asheville last summer, is it?" I asked.

"No, I've upgraded a bit since our last trip," he said with a laugh.

"I thought it looked a bit larger," I said.

"It is. This is an eight passenger plane. The Cessna 310 Crusader you flew in last year was a six seater. And this has jet engines not props. And best of all, it flies at 510 miles per hour. The Cessna maxed out at less than half of that. Take a look inside. I think you'll like it," Burt said.

I climbed into the plane while he finished his exterior inspection. Wow! This was nice. The seats were cream colored leather and each one was as wide and padded as a recliner. This ought to be good!

I climbed back down the stairs and noticed that the runway was no longer grass. It had been paved. Burt had made a lot of improvements over the past year.

"Why don't you and your guests park your cars in the hanger?" Burt said. "Same place as last time."

Ken pulled up in his truck just as I was getting back into the Boxster. I motioned to Ken to follow me. When we'd pulled into our parking spots, I pressed the batmobile button and put the top up on the Boxster. Best to keep out any critters while we were away.

Marsha and Ed, and Bella and Destiny arrived together. By 7:00 a.m. we'd all stowed our cars in the hanger and our gear in the plane. We were ready for takeoff!

Ken and I sat in the first two passenger seats, Marsha and Ed had the middle row and Bella and Destiny the next two. Each of us had a great window view. Captain Burt revved the engines and we literally jetted down the runway. Farmland and trees blurred by and we were airborne quickly.

Looking down, I could see the contours of the land. The farm fields on the rolling hills and valleys were freshly planted. Dense woodlands just coming into spring green haze bordered the fields. A herd of whitetail deer ran out from the edge of the woods and darted across a corn field.

In minutes the picture had expanded like a zoom-out camera lens. The fields were small patches now; the hills rolled on for miles. I could see a few country roads winding through them.

"St. Barths here we come!" Bella said.

Destiny applauded and we all joined in her enthusiasm.

"Tell us a little something about St. Barths, Karen. You've been there before, haven't you?" Marsha asked.

"I have, and I'm sure you're going to love it! Let's see, what can I tell you? Well, it's a French island, so you know the food is wonderful. There's lots of fresh fish, of course, and they fly in produce from the surrounding islands every day," I said. "And there's lots of good wine."

"Why do they fly in veggies? Why don't they grow them there?" Bella asked.

"Well, when you see the island, you'll know why. It's very mountainous. The island has lots of steep peaks, and the soil's too rocky to have any sort of farm except maybe a tiny plot for a family's use," I said. "But actually, that had an upside. Because they couldn't have big farms, they never had slaves on the island. Its heritage is mostly French settlers from Normandy and Brittany," I said.

"Tell us a little about the history of the island," Ed said.

"I'm glad you asked! I did a little research just for our trip. I can tell you that Christopher Columbus was the first European explorer to find the island in 1493. Remember, 'In 1492, Columbus sailed the ocean blue?' Well, apparently he was still sailing in 1493. He named the island St. Barthelemy, for his brother. There were fierce Carib Indians occupying the island when he got there. And the island had absolutely no fresh water. Not a single river. Still the same today," I said.

"So what do they do for water?" Bella asked. "Do they import it or use rain water?"

"I'm sure they used rain water for much of the island's history. But they've built a desalination plant on the island now," I said.

"So when did the French arrive?" Ken asked.

"Well, the French, the English, the Portuguese and the Spanish fought over the island for 150 years. The island has natural harbors, scalloped bays that are protected from rough seas by offshore coral reefs. The sailors used the harbors for refuge. It wasn't until 1648 that the first settlers came to the island. They were the French. For some reason, in 1784, King Louis XIV sold St. Barths to Sweden. That's why the capital of St. Barths is called Gustavia, after King Gustav III of Sweden."

"So, how long did Sweden have the island? You said it's French now, right?" Ed asked.

"Right. Well, the island was under Sweden's control for about 100 peaceful years. They built solid buildings, plotted out the city of Gustavia, and made the island a free port, which it still is today. But in 1877 the islanders voted to give the island back to France. And it's been a French Island ever since," I said.

"How big is the island?" Marsha asked.

"It's only about 18 square miles of land," I said.

"How many people live there?" Destiny asked.

"There are 8,000 people living on the island," I responded.

"I'd never heard of it," Bella said.

"Probably because there are no big planes that fly in there. The airstrip's too small to handle them. So it doesn't get too much publicity. Rockefeller started coming to the island and then a few rich tourists discovered it in the 1960's. Tourism grew in the 1980's and it's been growing ever since," I said.

"Sort of a shame in a way. I'd hate to see the natural beauty that made it a tourist destination destroyed by having too many people there," Ken said.

"Well, they're pretty smart about it. They have building restrictions that keep the density down. And they've made the ocean floor a protected nature preserve. And, with the tiny airstrip, it's harder to get to, so that limits the number of tourists, too. Hopefully, they'll find a balance that will support their economy without destroying the beauty," I said.

"What's that you're saying about a tiny airstrip?" Marsha asked.

"Oh, you've never seen anything like this, I'm sure. The airport is just beyond a mountain top on one of the few flat strips of land. You have to fly in through a narrow, mountain pass, and then immediately drop down to the runway and stop before you run into the ocean! It's pretty exciting. People actually drive up on the mountain road to watch the planes come in!" I said.

"Do planes ever go into the ocean?" Destiny asked.

"Don't worry. They have a strip of sand at the end of the runway to stop any planes from going into the ocean. And they hardly ever need to use it," I said with a chuckle. But I could see she was getting concerned so I added, "Captain Burt is flying us to St. Martin and we're chartering a smaller plane to fly us to St. Barths. The charter pilot flies into St. Barths all the time. He'll get us in safely."

That seemed to allay her concerns because she asked, cheerily, "What will we do for the whole week?"

"Oh, the beaches are the best! Remember, I told you about the scalloped bays the sailors used for refuge? Well, each one has a gorgeous sand beach. The mountains run down to the ocean along either side of these bays making for spectacu-lar views and privacy. And there are just a few hotels on each beach. The one we're going to is on Grand Cul-de-Sac Bay and has the best windsurfing on the island. It's on the northeast shore of the island, on the windward side. There's a barrier reef a mile off shore that keeps the breakers out, so you have great wind without the waves for terrific wind surfing!"

"I don't know how to wind surf," Destiny said.

"There'll be a teacher there. Probably a young French fellow just about your age," I said. That got her interest.

"What's our hotel like?" Bella asked.

"Well, we're right on the beach. We have three little bungalows just a few steps from the ocean. There's a little flower garden, a pool, and a great open-sided restaurant called Bobo's. They'll have coffee and croissants and yogurt for breakfast or hot chocolate if you'd like. And they serve the best lunches and dinners. You can take hikes on the hills around the bay, or go snorkeling, or just lie on the beach and read," I said.

"That sounds so good," Marsha said.

Gradually our chatter subsided and we each drifted into our own thoughts. Mine shifted between the adventures to come and what we'd just been through.

Marsha's mind must have been drifting along the same lines because she said, "Karen, what's happening with that fellow you and Ken found, Ron Reilley. Is he still in the hospital?"

"I talked to his sister yesterday. Ron's out of the hospital and he's going to stay with her for a while," I said. "Detective Cavanaugh contacted the fellow who's making the settlement payments so they'll be coming to the real Ron Reilley now. They hope that eventually Ron will be able to go back to work," I said.

"I hope he's able to let go of all that misplaced anger. Those emails he sent to Wilbur were pretty awful. Johnny told me about them," Marsha said.

"His sister told me that Ron had dropped that grudge against Wilbur a long time ago. Isolde wanted us to believe Ron was angry with Wilbur. She exaggerated that story for her own purposes. It was Isolde and Sol Sneed who sent those emails to Wilbur using Ron's name so that we'd believe Ron was the one responsible for Wilbur's death," I said.

"For all that planning, dropping a bronze statue on Wilbur seems sort of spontaneous and risky," Ken said.

"I think it was. Isolde and Wilbur had just had a fight about the patent. I think she just snapped when she saw him standing there below her at the gallery. I expect Isolde and Sol were really planning something more methodical, like an accident at the lab."

"How's Johnny doing?" Ken asked.

"I talked to him last night after we heard what happened to you and Ken," Marsha said. "Johnny's going to talk to the patent attorney today to let him know about Isolde and to get the patent changed to Wilbur's Estate. Johnny plans to license the patent for biofuel production. He said that's what his uncle would have wanted," Marsha said.

"Did you ever hear what happened to Zay Lately?" Bella asked.

"Yes. It turns out that Zay had gone off her meds. She had a few bumps and bruises from the crash but nothing too serious. The doctors expect her to make a full recovery now that she's back on her medicines," I said.

"And our insurance is covering the damage to the gallery. The repairs are already underway," Ed said.

"That's great!" I said.

The morning flew by, both literally and figuratively. By noon, we'd started our descent. We broke through the clouds to see gorgeous turquoise water. A large island dotted with red tiled roofs was right below us. Boats were anchored off shore. "That large island must be St. Martin," I said. "We'll switch planes and be on St. Barths in no time at all!"

Chapter Fourteen

Feet in the Sand

Thursday Afternoon

I pressed my bare feet into the warm sand. Ken was sitting across from me. Marsha, Ed, Bella and Destiny were sitting in the other chairs around our table. It was noon on Thursday and we were celebrating our first full day on the island with lunch at The Lafayette Club. To say The Lafayette Club was the best dining experience on St. Barths doesn't say enough. It was one of the best in the world. Not only is the food fantastic, the setting is as relaxed as it is beautiful.

We had sun on our backs and chilled champagne in our glasses. There are only a dozen tables at this beachside restaurant each with a perfect view of the clear turquoise water of Grand Cul-de-Sac Bay. The water's edge was only 25 feet from us and gentle waves lapped the smooth sand beach. Windsurfers, with their brilliant colored sails and acrobatic feats, were putting on quite a show.

We clinked our glasses, sipped bubbly and laughed. Over the next hour, our waiter brought us shrimp appetizers, followed by fresh lobster, fresh baked French bread and salad, all served with a buttery chardonnay.

"What more could we ask for?" Bella said.

"It's a bit of paradise isn't it?" I replied.

"I'm glad we could all share it together," Ken said.

"I just wish Johnny could be here with us," I said. "I talked to him last night though."

"Oh, how's he doing?" Marsha asked.

"Really, pretty well, I think. The patent attorney has another client who wants to license Johnny's patent. He should have the patent approved in a few months," I said.

"That's great," Ed said.

"And, Johnny's decided to donate a conservation easement to the JDCF so that Wilbur's land will be preserved for future generations," I said.

"What about the development that he and Bull were working on?" Bella asked.

"Bull's moving the development to a flat stretch of land along the new route for Highway 20. Apparently, he had this as a backup plan all along. And it's only a few miles away so all of his marketing studies and design plans will work on that site just as well," I said.

"So he's not mad at Johnny?" Marsha asked.

"No. Johnny said Bull was actually happy because he plans to partner with the Historical Society and a Native American Tribal Association on the Indian Museum portion of the development. The tribe can direct some of their casino money into the museum to create more awareness of the Native American history and culture in the Midwest," I said.

"That's a great idea!" Ken said. "It's time we studied the full history of our area, not just the history of European settlement."

"And Johnny will still be living in his home and painting those wonderful views from Horseshoe Mound," Marsha said.

"Talk about painting, how's your new orchid painting coming along?" Ed asked me.

"Great! It should be done in June. Then I'm going to work on two smaller companion paintings. I've been invited to display a suite of orchid paintings at next year's orchid show at Longwood Gardens," I said.

"An orchid show? That sounds fabulous! Where is it?" Bella asked.

"In Kennett Square, Pennsylvania," I said. I was met by questioning looks. "It's near Wilmington, Delaware," I said.

"When is the show?" Marsha asked.

"In March," I said.

"Well, I think we should all go!" Ken said and raised his glass.

We all raised our glasses to meet his and toasted.

"Sounds great! Let's plan on it!" I said.

Chocolate Molten Torte

4 ounces semi-sweet chocolate
4 ounces unsweetened chocolate
¾ cup unsalted butter
3 egg yolks
3 whole eggs
¾ cup sugar
¾ cup all purpose flour

Whipped Cream or Ice Cream

Butter 10 four-ounce ceramic ramekins and dust with flour. Melt butter and chocolate, set aside and let cool. In a mixing bowl, use electric mixer to combine eggs and sugar until pale yellow batter holds shape and forms ribbon on beaters. Blend flour into egg-sugar mixture with the mixer for 3 minutes. Add chocolate mixture, being careful to incorporate everything; mix for 2 more minutes. Pour about 3 ounces of batter into each ramekin filling the ramekins ¾ to the top, and refrigerate for 1 hour.

Preheat oven to 475 degrees.

Bake ramekins on a cookie sheet for 10 minutes or until they are puffed up and don't jiggle when moved. Remove from oven and from the ramekins and serve immediately.

Serve with whipped cream or ice cream.

Serves 10

Bella's Best Chocolate Brownies

2 sticks butter
4 squares unsweetened baking chocolate
2 cups sugar
4 large eggs
1 ½ cups flour
½ teaspoon salt
1 teaspoon baking powder
2 teaspoons vanilla
2 cups chopped walnuts

Preheat oven to 350 degrees.

Melt the butter and chocolate. In separate bowl, mix salt and baking powder into flour. Add sugar, eggs and vanilla to chocolate/butter mixture and mix well by hand. Mix in walnuts. Grease and flour two 9 inch by 9 inch baking pans. Divide batter evenly between the two pans.

Bake for 40 minutes.

Frosting

3 squares unsweetened baking chocolate
4 tablespoons butter
3 cups powdered sugar
Dash vanilla
¼ cup milk (more or less as needed)

Melt chocolate and butter together. Stir in powdered sugar and vanilla. Add milk to spreadable consistency

Makes 2 dozen brownies

Mailing List

To receive your notice of the next Karen Prince Mystery

Send your name and address to:

Galena Publishing
P.O. Box 18
Galena, Illinois 61036

Or email: **skprincipe@aol.com.** You can send your email address if you would prefer to be notified electronically.

You can use this page, or a copy of it:

Name: _____

Street Address: _____

City, State and Zip code: _____

Email Address: _____

ORDER FORM for AUTOGRAPHED BOOKS

1st Book: **Murder in Galena**

2nd Book: **Murder on the Mississippi**

3rd Book: **Murder at Galena Stables**

4th Book: **Murder at Galena Gallery**

Please send me:

_____ autographed copies of Murder in Galena

_____ autographed copies of Murder on the Mississippi

_____ autographed copies of Murder at Galena Stables

_____ autographed copies of Murder at Galena Gallery

I enclosed $15.50 for each book or $14.50 each for 2 or more books.

Please make check payable to: Galena Publishing.

Shipping Charges are $3.50 per order.

Please add 6.25% sales tax if shipped to an Illinois address.

Send my books to:

Name: _____

Street Address: _____

City and State: _____

Zip Code: _____

Please autograph my books to: _____

_____

Mail this form to: Galena Publishing
P.O. Box 18
Galena, Illinois 61036

About the Author

Sandra Principe lives with her husband in the countryside near Galena. A Chicago lawyer for 20 years, she moved to the Galena area in 1996 to write and paint. She received her Bachelor of Science in English Education and her Juris Doctorate Degree from the University of Wisconsin, Madison.

Ms. Principe's paintings have been shown in galleries and museums across the country from Florida to California. This novel is a unique combination of her special knowledge of Galena, painting, mysteries and travel. Ms. Principe's first mystery, Murder in Galena, was published in 2003. Her second mystery, Murder on the Mississippi, was published in 2005. The third book, Murder at Galena Stables, was published in 2007. This is the fourth book in the Karen Prince Galena Mystery Series.

See Sandra Principe's paintings
and learn more about her work at:

www.sandraprincipe.com

Email: skprincipe@aol.com